Swing
State

A NOVEL BY

Michael T. Fournier

THREE ROOMS PRESS

NEW YORK

Swing State
A novel by Michael T. Fournier

First printing

ISBN: 978-1-941110-08-9
Library of Congress Control Number: 2014937998

AUTHOR PHOTOS:
Rebecca S. Griffin

COVER AND INTERIOR DESIGN:
KG Design International
www.katgeorges.com

DISTRIBUTED BY:
PGW/Perseus
www.pgw.com

Three Rooms Press
New York, NY
www.threeroomspress.com

Sandra Styrna Griffin
February 12, 1952 – December 21, 2011

Gray eidolon! so quickly gone
    When eyes, that make thee, onward move;
Whose vast pretense of permanence
    A little progress can disprove!

John Townsend Trowbridge
"The Old Man of the Mountain"

before after

Swing
State

1.

Empty restaurant. Hot out. Indian summer. Twenty in quarters lasted Roy weeks.

He lost the first two or three. Sometimes for real. Getting warmed up. The feel of the cue. Each one different. Wanted his own. But couldn't afford one. And no one would play him. But knew a few of the bar's. Recognized them.

After two or three he didn't pay. He started small. Played for next game. Made some lucky play. Oops. How did I do that? Kids without faces, always the same. Never any good.

Nothing to do there. Afghanistan. Hurry up and wait. Got good fast. Came back with skills. Both hands. Kids too stupid to realize. Anyone playing for money thinks they can beat you. But he didn't think. He knew. And he did. Fuck them when they got pissed.

Except the nights with no one there. Middle of the month, Tuesday. Sox on TV. One couple at the bar. Jap walked the bases loaded. Again.

Empty restaurant. Hot out. Saw river swimming on the walk over. Kids bridge jumping. Charcoal. Meat. No bugs. Cold one on the porch. If you had one. He didn't. Kitchen, one room.

Hamburger Helper. But a porch. A grill. He wouldn't play pool. Game on the radio. Cold ones in a cooler.

No one to see his row of next game quarters. The guy, the fuck was his name? Patterson? Or was the lady Patterson? He brought the first one. Here you go, Roy. Slow night. On the house.

First beer tasted good. Cold. It'd be better outside. Drink it in the weather. Not AC. But better in the AC than in his apartment. In front of a box fan. He'd tried. Game on the radio. Six pack. Fan didn't help. Still felt the heat. Drinking by himself in front of a fan.

Racked 'em. No one around. He'd play himself. Do challenges. Stripes had to hit one bumper. Solids, another ball. If someone came he'd stop. Play lefty. Miss a few.

Patterson still standing there. I hope you get to play someone, Roy.

Me too. If not, I'll practice.

It'll be cheaper if there's other people.

Patterson, the lady, she'd say something about gambling being illegal. He knew the type. Didn't want that nonsense in her bar. But Patterson. He knew. Didn't mind. Liked the guy.

Want to play?

I'd love to. But it's my bar. I owe you a game, tell you what.

Roy respected that. Business. And she'd freak out. Be like don't play pool with customers. All right, Roy said. Say when.

I'm not that good, Patterson said. Smart. He owned the place, had the table. Probably played before work, after.

The door opened. Four people came in. Here we go, Patterson said. He walked to the altar by the door. They talked. Roy couldn't hear, but saw them laugh. Patterson knew what to say. The people went to the bar, Patterson smiling, pulling taps. Shaking shakers.

Drinks. Cold. Must feel good. To sit at a bar and talk. With friends.

Jap gave up a single on TV. Two runs scored. Fucking Sox. Solid in the corner. Hit another ball. Hard. A stripe hit a solid in front of the pocket and in. He swallowed beer. Still cold. Glass sweat. Radio jazz. No good music. Not until late night, after dinner. Bar crowd. Sometimes. Never Korn or Disturbed or Ministry. Stuff they played overseas. Scare factor. Probably not good for a bar. But AC/DC. People liked them. Reminded him. When he drove he heard them a lot. Good music for it. But didn't mind not driving. Could walk everywhere. A little slow. Leg still not right. Stronger every day. But still not the same.

Solids lining up just right. An accident. Some games were like that. Didn't have to do much work. Every time Roy hit a stripe a solid bounced right. Good shots.

Stripes into solids. Every time. Didn't miss. Stripes didn't have a chance. Eight ball in. Easy. Racked them again, more quarters. Paid. Solids had to hit two balls first now. Stripes, still one bumper. Handicap. Solids doing so good, had to even it.

Jap got out of the inning somehow. Commercial. People laughing, drinking beer on TV. Looked good. His was still cold. Might have one more. First one free. On the house. Then back. Nothing to do but sit in front of a box fan and listen to the game. No people. Too hot. In their cars, on their porches.

Lefty next. Another beer. He tried hard lefty. Wasn't great. Play games with people lefty. Then for money. Switch hands.

On TV Ortiz struck out. Ended the inning. Yelled at the ump. Never used to, Ortiz. Used to mash. Roy saw it all. 2004, 2007. And the Bruins. Overseas for that. Heard the next day. Peck, it was. No radios on patrol. Your team, Peck said, they won. Peck who didn't like baseball. Or hockey. Wasn't his fault. From the south. They didn't care. There was Texas, their teams. Rangers. Astros. And Florida. New ones: Marlins, Rays. Or Atlanta. But instead Peck liked football. Bama, Cowboys. His teams. Roy liked football. Patriots. Peck got mad at him. Cowboys, Peck said. But Peck got it. Your Bruins, they won last night. Roy thought about drinking beers, going into his yard and yelling BRUINS. How the neighbors would be pissed. His Auntie Blake. He wouldn't care. BRUINS.

He missed Peck. The star on the side of his helmet. Cowboys, Peck said. No Patriots. Cowboys.

Patterson behind the bar with his good posture. Made him look alert. Another one, Roy?

Yessir.

Patterson pulled the Venerable tap.

Looks like you're doing trick shots over there.

Stripes hit a bumper, solid two balls. Tried just one but it was too easy. Might play lefty next.

It's amazing, Roy. You play better with your left hand than most people play with their right.

Never used to be able to.

Patterson put his beer down on the bar. Here you go. Good luck with the left hand.

Thanks.

Roy waited at the table. Racked them again.

On TV, the Jap walked another one. Always doing that. Load the bases, three strikeouts in a row. Some bullshit. Honor. They played different. Had to think about the opponent. Be respectful. Strikeouts. One man against the other. Pitcher against hitter. No grounders, no pop ups. Better man wins. He didn't agree. The opponent, humiliate them. Make them feel like shit. Get them down. Show them pictures. You see this? You know him? Your friend, this guy? He squealed like a pig when we did that. You know what a pig is? A fuckin' disgusting animal. Filthy. That's what he sounded like. An animal who sticks his nose in his own shit. Eats it. We don't have a broom in this tent. Lucky for you because you'd sweep all day. No hands. But we think you can do a 'persination of a pig. Think you can do that? Or do we need a broom? Either way, your ass is grass. You know what grass is? Ever seen any? Probably not. But you better understand what it means when I say I'm the lawnmower. Got me?

Now do a pig 'persination.

Humiliated. Like the other day. Walked down to the store. Ran out of food. Beans, ramen. All he could afford.

L'il Bee. Beer in the cooler. And dusty cans on shelves. Probably more expensive than the grocery store. But too far to walk.

Guy behind the counter put the cans and noodles in a plastic bag.

Walked back outside.

Explosion.

Was on his stomach before he could think about it. Was like that. Overseas. No time to think. Just react. Save your ass. Your buddies. Like that time. In the back of the truck. The clouds. Metal in his mouth.

Any loud noise, on the ground. Incoming. No time to think. Get down. Grenades, mortars, guns. Except none in fucking Armbrister, New Hampshire. Just some little bitch. And her fire-works. Over by the dumpster. Picked himself up off the ground. She didn't look legal. Flannel shirt, long hair. Denim jacket. Big.

Tough-looking. Okay tits. Holding a paper bag. Pointing. Laughing. Oh, man. You shoulda seen yourself! You looked pretty stupid, you know that? Hahahaha. It's just a Silver Salute! Shit, these aren't even M-80s.

Couldn't get mad. Hit a girl. Say anything. But he felt it. Face flushed. Just some girl. Didn't know him. What he did. Overseas. No one did. He hoped.

2.

Testing. Hey, testing.

Testes. Hey, testes. One two three.

Testes. One two.

* * *

(sound of explosion)

Holy FUCK was that loud!

* * *

(sound of explosion)

I don't think that one was as good. Hold on—

* * *

Nope. Silver Salutes aren't as good as M-80s.

Not even close. This tape proves it.

* * *

I'm walking home.

I've never had one of these things before. It was in a car.

I guess maybe I shouldn't say that. I should say it was on the road. Or in front of my mom's house.

Besides, I have a good hiding place. I keep all my stuff there.

But if you're listening, Ross: FUCK OFF. YOU'RE AN ASSHOLE.

And if you're still listening: I KNOW WHERE YOU KEEP YOUR SHIT.

Okay, this was just sitting there on the front seat.

Nothing on here was any good. I listened before I started. Some lawyer or something. Boring.

Ding woulda given me like a few M-80s or whatever for this. Six months ago that would've been cool, but now not so much. I mean, I love blowing shit up. It rules. But I'd rather get paid. Then I can get my own place.

* * *

I have a bunch of different places. Like the police station parking lot. That's a good spot. People think their stuff is safe because it's parked out front. But it's not like the cops are looking out the windows. They're doing cop stuff. So that's where I get wallets. Phones. GPSs. Ding likes those. Doesn't give me much, but I always get something. Says everyone uses them. Especially if they have a cord.

* * *

My voice sounds funny on here. Like tough. Good.

* * *

This is Dixon Dove. You are listening to the rock of New Hampshire. WNAH. Wilburton.

The rock of northern New Hampshire! WNAH. Wilburton!

* * *

I don't have the right voice for that.

* * *

I'm almost home.

Today's Monday, so Mom does the mill, then the register at the L'il Bee. She'll get home like 11:30.

Don probably has money left from his check, so he'll be at the bar.

Ross will be at practice.

Wonder what's in the freezer.

* * *

It's Tuesday now.

I didn't see anyone.

Mom's always yelling. Telling me I'm not going to make anything of myself if I don't go to school. Well, she went and look where it got her: the mill, and behind the cash register of a convenience store. And Don got his diploma. He went to Iraq and Afghanistan.

Mom was like there are always nursing jobs. So I tried those classes. No way. Anatomy sucks. And besides, what kind of job would that be? Wiping asses. Mom's pissed I quit, but whatever.

My stupid brother is gonna go to college. Sometimes Coach comes around with recruiters. Mom takes time off work, and Don stops drinking. I have to clean before they come. Ross stops smoking so he doesn't stink or sound stupid.

How do they not notice? Maybe they don't care. I don't know how he's gonna get through college if he can't smoke. Drug tests and all that.

Recruiters come and tell him he's gonna be a star. Schools far away. Michigan and Ohio and Wisconsin. After they leave I tell him how much it's gonna suck to be in the middle of nowhere but I'm just kidding. Kinda. I'd rather be someplace where no one knows me than in Armbrister. It's not like I'm stupid. You beat up a few boys and you get a reputation.

Well, fine. I'm a bitch. Whatever.

* * *

School today was boring. Just like it always is. I wish I could drop out. I mean, I could, but I'd have to get a job. I'd turn into my mom. Part-time, cool. But I don't wanna be like her.

Maybe I should have done voc. Stuck to nursing. But I hate it. And I hate cars, and cooking, and building stuff.

I thought about joining up. Going places. Seeing the world. But Afghanistan is probably worse than Armbrister. Getting shot at? No way.

I mean, I could blow stuff up over there. That'd be cool. They have grenades and stuff. Explode some trucks. Or buildings. Demolition. But I'd come back, if I lived through it, and not have anything to do all over again. Like the guy I see walking around the common. Or Don. Jesus, all he does is drink. The bar, the couch, wherever. He tells Mom he's looking for jobs but then he sits and watches TV all day and gets wasted.

I dunno if he used to be like this before he went, but he's always giving me shit like he's my dad or something. But I should be glad. If it wasn't for him I'd still be trading GPSs for fireworks instead of saving to get out of here.

* * *

I was bored at lunch today. I can't believe kids listen to me when I tell them to give me cash. What a bunch of idiots! But they're scared of me, so they do, even though I'm kidding. Or at least half-kidding. Hahaha.

There's this skinny kid with glasses who starts to give me cash now before I even say anything to him. He just, like, gives it to me. And the tall kid who shakes when I come over. I haven't seen the fat kid who always brings the same sandwich for a while.

* * *

I got an iPod today. One of the little ones. Ding loves those. He'll give me some cash.

A watch, too. Looks like gold. Just sitting there in an SUV. Mass plates. That'll teach a Masshole. Live free or die, bitch!

* * *

I went to the parking lot to see if Ding was there. He wasn't. So I went up to the quarry.

All the usual people were there, sitting around, drinking beers, and smoking butts. Someone brought a radio, playing WNAH. Block Party Weekend. Ozzy doing "Crazy Train."

The new girl was up there. I've seen her around. She's in my English class. She sits way up front. I saw her looking at me when I came in a few times. Her name's Mary.

Steve said you want a beer, Dixon? I said yeah, and he threw me a can of Venerable.

He said gonna jump today?

I said if I was gonna, I wouldn't wait until it got cold out. And I'd bring a fucking towel.

They all started laughing. Steve sat there stroking his shitty moustache like he always does. He said hey, Earl, she's got you there.

Earl was all wet, shivering with no shirt on. He gave me the finger and said why don't you just take your shirt off and jump in?

I was like yeah, you'd like that. You'd go home and spank it.

They all laughed. Even Mary.

Earl said I only spank it to girls with tits.

I was like whatever. I have great tits and I know it. And I know how to use them.

Steve said you gonna open that beer?

I sat next to him on the granite slab and opened it.

He said whatcha doing up here? You're not jumping.

I said looking for Ding.

Steve goes I heard he might have some M-80s.

I said I'm not into those any more.

He said Silver Salutes?

I said no, I'm trying to make some cash.

He nodded and said that's cool. Then he asked about my brother. I told him that Ross was doing football.

Steve said Ross used to hang out up there a lot. At the quarries. I told Steve about Ross's practices.

Earl came over and put a shirt on. He was drinking a beer and shivering. He said what's up, Dixon?

I said same shit.

He told me he applied over at the mill.

Steve started laughing at him and said he'd never get in.

Earl was like fuck you.

Mary came over and asked Steve for a beer.

While he was getting one out of the case she was like hey, aren't you in my English class?

I was like oh yeah, I guess so.

She sat down on the slab and said that class is pretty cool. I was like yeah, even though I never pay attention. I don't like reading.

Earl and Steve were arguing about the mill.

Mary said what are you guys talking about?

Steve pointed at Earl and was like this guy thinks he's gonna work at the mill.

Earl said I put in an application. He wasn't shivering anymore.

Steve stroked his shitty mustache. He said everyone wants to get in at the mill. Even though they used to pay fifteen and now they pay nine.

I watched Mary's eyes get all big. She was like why did they do that?

Steve said there's less jobs in town. They can pay whatever they want.

Earl said nine isn't bad.

I was like you're gonna get stuck here.

He said maybe I wanna get stuck, you ever think of that?

Steve looked at Mary and said Dixon's not gonna get stuck. Her brother's a big football star.

She looked at me and I kinda shrugged.

Steve asked if he knew where he was gonna go for school. I said not yet.

Earl said when he goes pro you're gonna have it made.

I was like whatever and took a big haul off my beer.

I burped. It was a good one. Everyone clapped and laughed.

Steve said you gonna go to the game this weekend? Cheer on your brother? I told him I didn't know. Then I told them I had to go.

Before I left I said hey, Mary, see you in class.

I don't know how much a pro football player makes. I'll have to find out. That means the library tomorrow.

3.

THIRTY-ONE SECONDS TO GO. FOURTH AND one on the Schaferville twenty.

The bleachers tremored under Zachariah Tietz's feet. Not normal tremors—he'd been to enough games to know the feel of a game on the line—but tremors like something was wrong. Like the bleachers were going to collapse.

He looked to see if his father had noticed. But Paul Tietz, naked from the waist up, painted white with a sky blue "A" covering his long face, clapped cupped hands and chanted along with the crowd—ARM! BRIS! TER! ARM! BRIS! TER!—oblivious to the distress of both the bleachers beneath his feet and his son, painted in his mirror image.

Homecoming meant spectators who hadn't been to a game in twenty years or more, and thus hadn't seen painted Paul Tietz and son, or heard any of Paul's stories of his Armbrister High glory days. After brief introductions, two towering men with huge hands and boozy breath clapped Zachariah on his flabby back with enough force to bruise: *Attaboy. A fan for life. Lookit that paint!*

Zachariah knew the story by heart: his dad had been on the field when Armbrister had won its lone state championship, in the nineties. Paul, of course, neglected to mention the star back twisted his ankle in a celebratory pigpile following the game-clinching interception against Manchester West, leaving a gap that would have been filled by a replacement player had he, Paul Tietz, third-string kick holder, not heroically run onto the field to take a knee for the good of the team.

He'd heard the stories about the team dozens of times. One of his father's favorites worried him: the epic tale of Roger Conroy's ninety-one yard Hail Mary on Thanksgiving to beat Schaferville at the end of regulation—also known as "The Greatest Play in Armbrister Sports History." Zachariah had been there in the stands with his father, but he had been three years old and had no memory of the day, the game, of Conroy hoisted onto shoulders in the middle of the field. One of his father's favorite photos was of that day: Paul and a chubby Zachariah, painted blue, cheering the victory.

His father's description of "The Play" always included the bleachers swaying fit to collapse. Thought they'd come down, he always said (and said earlier in the game to the men in the stands). But if we'd been killed right there we would have died with smiles on our faces.

On the field, Schaferville's defense bumbled around the line of scrimmage as the crowd howled. The coach, across the field from where they sat, held his hands in a "T."

"See that? They had to stop because of us! Time out! Because of the fans!"

The men around them cheered Paul Tietz. The crowd's "ARM! BRIS! TER!" chant continued unabated all around. One of the men began stomping his feet on the last syllable for added emphasis. Zachariah felt his painted breasts—his tietz, as that girl Dixon called them—jiggle against his chest.

I'm going to die, Zachariah thought. None of my game shows will ever be on TV. I will never own a bakery. I'm going to die.

His father clapped and yelled.

During the week, Paul drank beer after beer and watched sports on TV when he got home from the mill. He only watched the news on game night, hoping one of the newscasters would cut to the stands, where he and Zachariah, painted, cheered on the team. They weren't shown often, for which Zachariah was grateful; one of the rotating cast of older kids in the voc wing, on Mondays after he and his father were shown, would inevitably have something to say about his television celebrity as they hipchecked him or wrenched his monogrammed L.L.Bean backpack from his shoulders and emptied it onto the floor or shook him down for money he never had. Zachariah wondered how they knew—what were they watching the news for, anyway?—and held his breath on the couch after the game every week, hoping for a reprieve.

He wanted to stay home and work on *Love Balloon*. Or make bread. But he couldn't. He had to go to games with his father. He couldn't imagine what would happen if he said he didn't want to go.

On the field, the ref blew his whistle.

His father leaned over. Spittle flew from his lips as he yelled over the din of the crowd: "WHAT ARE THEY GONNA DO?"

Zachariah said nothing.

His father: "FOURTH AND ONE. WHAT ARE THEY GONNA DO?"

"Sneak?"

"THEY EXPECT THAT!"

"Put that defensive lineman in there," one of the men said. "The kid who's gonna be pro. Run a play behind him. What's that kid's name again?"

The teams formed at the line of scrimmage. Zachariah saw the Armbrister quarterback, Brandon Fahey, pointing at the line, waving his hands.

"WHAT ARE THEY GONNA DO?"

Zachariah first envisioned the wrong answer. His dad getting mad that he'd been shown up "in front of friends"—the kind of friends he made every week at games with his flask and boasts—and seeing him take the soccer sock of tennis balls from the closet afterward.

Then he imagined the bleachers groaning first to one side, then the other, before teetering and finally collapsing in a giant pile of sharp edges and flailing limbs, a pointed steel beam slowly pushing through his stomach as he screamed.

"THAT'S RIGHT. THEY'LL PASS!"

The men nodded.

Paul glowered at his son.

Fahey dropped back with the snap and lobbed a lazy arc to MacPhail, the tight end, who pulled the ball to his chest and stutter-stepped out of bounds to stop the clock.

First down.

The crowd roared.

How could they not notice the bleachers?

"PERFECT. STOP THE CLOCK. FOUR MORE."

The bleachers lurched.

Zachariah hoped his death would be quick and painless.

A heavy hand slammed into his back.

"Some game, ain't it?"

"Yes, sir," Zachariah said, thinking: we'll all be dead in a minute.

"Games like this make you proud to be a Spartans fan!"

Zachariah thought that if he lived, he'd make a challenge on *Love Balloon*: the Drunk Guy Relay. Run an obstacle course of mental challenges and then make it through a series of collapsing bleachers.

His father leaned over to them.

"WHAT'S IT GONNA BE?"

It doesn't matter, Zachariah thought. They'd all be dead. But he wanted the last few minutes of his life to be as painless as possible. So:

"First down," he said. "They'll try for the end zone because they have three more after this. An incomplete stops the clock."

The man who thumped Zachariah's back grinned and nodded. "You started him early," the man yelled to Paul. "Fan for life."

Paul nodded and passed the man his flask. He smiled briefly at Zachariah.

Both teams huddled up. Twenty-seven seconds.

Fahey feinted forward with the snap, then dropped back. He loosed a wobbling spiral.

The bleachers, fuse of expectation lit, fell silent.

This is it, Zachariah thought. If he catches the ball—who is that? Laramore—everyone will yell and clap and stomp. There's no way the bleachers will hold. We're right in the middle. I'll fall, then I'll be crushed by everyone landing on me. And there's going to be metal. Sharp pointy metal.

Maybe he'll drop it.

But then it'll happen all over again, second and goal. And everyone will be more excited.

An interception, though.

Yeah. An interception.

His father would spend the rest of the afternoon on the couch, drinking beer, flipping channels looking for sports. Maybe a baseball game, maybe golf. It didn't matter. His disappointment would be so great that he'd watch whatever was on. Paul got sad when Armbrister lost. He got mad when Zachariah messed up stats or called plays incorrectly. Zachariah hadn't been saying anything when he wasn't sure, which worked.

Once his dad passed out, Zachariah would be free to work on *Love Balloon*. He knew the ending, but he had to figure out the rest.

So that's it, he thought. *An interception, then* Love Balloon.

The ball wobbled through the air.

Laramore stopped his route and poised himself to make the catch.

The crowd waited to explode and kill Zachariah Tietz.

Behind Laramore, pistoning arms and legs in crimson and white.

Zachariah's eyes widened.

Fahey hadn't seen the safety.

Laramore, frozen, as the piston raced past him up the sideline.

The small throng across the field in the away bleachers erupted.

The men around Zachariah stood silent and motionless.

Schaferville's safety slowed as he approached the end zone. He held the ball aloft and high-stepped in.

Zachariah felt a grin widening across his face. He looked down quickly. The men around him, his father—none of them could see.

It was hard to make the grin go away. After all, it wasn't every day that he, Zachariah Tietz, decided a game, and the fate of everyone in the bleachers, with his mind.

* * *

"Shoulda known the goddamn shafety wash gonna be there," Paul said on the ride home. "Sheriously, he'sh the only good guy on the whole team.

"Yeah," Zachariah said. He knew what happened didn't make sense, but it had happened. He had seen the imminent death of everyone in the stands, and, through the power of his mind, prevented it.

Maybe his new talent had something to do with his weight gain, which had been stunning in its immediacy. In the course of a few months—summer vacation—he had ballooned. His father, between beers, told him to *go outside and get some exercise, goddammit.* Zachariah thought he got plenty. He rode his bike around, kicked a soccer ball against the cinderblock wall of the school toolshed (this despite what happened to him on the field). But still, his T-shirts began to hug him like he was a sausage, and his underwear cut off circulation to his legs.

The upside—if there was one—was his new wardrobe. He'd needed one. Until last year, he hadn't thought of his clothes at all. But after the soccer field incident his clothes drew attention. His sweaters and T-shirts and cords. He couldn't walk down the hall without someone picking on him. It didn't matter that he'd known some of his tormentors since preschool.

And that was all before his weight gain.

His dad begrudgingly gave him a hundred dollars. Zachariah took it to the thrift store, hoping no one would be there to witness him scouring the racks for clothing that fit. Maybe his powers (as he had already come to think of them) had been active even then: it felt inevitable that someone would be there to make fun of him during the Thrift Store Clothing Challenge. But no one appeared to harass him. Was it because he had used his powers? Because, as he shopped for XXL clothes bearing no logos, in an attempt to render himself invisible, he had thought *I don't want anyone to see me?*

He hoped so. Even though it felt impossible.

When else had he used his powers? And how often was he allowed to use them? He thought back. At some point during the school year he must've thought *I wish they'd leave me alone* when he was being picked on in the hallways. His new clothes didn't make him invisible, as he had hoped: he was the center of unwanted attention everywhere he went. If he didn't know better—and maybe he didn't—he'd say their plainness magnified his abuse. This girl named Dixon, who scared the crap out of him, whose weird burnt smell preceded her, had begun to notice and summarily harass him. Maybe his plain clothes hadn't drawn enough attention away from his new man boobs, which, he thought with a mixture of bemusement and satisfaction, were bigger than hers. Except she never said boobs. She found out his whole name somehow—even though he only knew her first name, Dixon—and called them his "tietz." Once she began her serial torture, with kids chanting his name as they passed, he wondered how he never saw it coming, that one day he'd get fat ("it happens, though usually in girls," the doctor had said) and his last name would define one of his most prominent physical features.

As Dixon leaned in and twisted his tietz to what felt like a breaking point, that unidentified but burnt smell overpowering his nostrils, her face hovered only inches from his, sneering. "You can't fight me because I'm a girl," she had said one of the first times. "If you hit a girl you're a piece of shit and everyone will know it." The thought of fighting back hadn't occurred to him until she mentioned it. He had no idea how. But he knew what she said was true. He was having a hard enough time already, navigating the new voc halls like a game show challenge with his new, clumsy body. The last thing he wanted was attention. And hitting a girl—even one who deserved it—would call just that sort of attention to him and make his life even worse.

Another time, as she twisted, she leaned in, burnt smell enveloping him, and said, "You're a perv, aren't you? You want to kiss me. I can tell."

He hadn't—until she mentioned it. And he wasn't sure he really wanted to. But who else would he kiss? Girls didn't know he was alive. She showed him more attention than anyone in school, not counting teachers.

Kids passing chanting tietz, tietz.

"Well?"

"Uh," he said. "I, uh . . ."

"Or maybe you're growing your own set of tietz so you can feel them." She paused. "Do you want to feel mine?"

She jutted her chest toward him.

He felt his face flush. And he felt himself getting hard down there.

Oh no, he thought. Not now.

"Do you?"

"Uh. Um . . ."

"You're always looking at them."

Usually when she finished twisting she heaved him backward. That time, though, she simply stopped. She was taller than him by a good six inches and looked silently down on him as she drew her hands back. He hoped she wouldn't notice he was hard. And he hoped she would.

She whispered "Tietz, you're a perv."

The next time, it was back to normal: can't hit a girl, a pinwheeling dismissal from her grasp that left him sprawled in the middle of the hall as people passing kicked him on their way to class. Sometimes now he got hard just thinking about it.

If he'd had powers then, things would have been different. So he'd have to find a way to test them out.

His dad pulled into the driveway.

"Shabout time for dinner," he said.

Zachariah could count the number of times his father had cooked since his mom left. Each time involved a grill. "I'll make us calzones," he said.

4.

Walking around the common, then to the woods.

Roy used to think he'd go someplace else. Maybe Boston. Liked it there. Went for games. Sox, Bruins. Big town. Everyone said walking city. Small. But it wasn't. Big. Walk all day. Roads in grids. Up and down. Learn every street, store. Restaurant. More than three there.

Now he couldn't go. Too much.

When Roy got back from Afghanistan Artie McCoy said hey I got these Sox tickets. Artie. Went to high school together. Moved to Wilburton. Girlfriend knocked up. Got a job. Garage in Schaferville. Still making jokes. Most people didn't. Not any more. But Artie did. The guys, they would have loved him.

They took his Mustang down. Awesome. 93 South, through Concord, past the Old Man of the Mountain. Where he used to be. Remembered the day he fell. His Auntie Blake said Royal, look at the paper. Ol' Stoney is gone.

That game Ortiz struck out four times. Golden Sombrero. Sox lost but he and Artie drank beer in plastic cups. Checked out tits and asses. Good to be back. Not warm enough to take his jacket off. But good to be there.

After, they had a few beers. Basement bar down the street. Cheaper than inside. Artie said next time a flask. TV replays of the strikeouts they barely saw from the bleachers.

Artie thought getting beers would help. People would leave while they drank, he said. But they went back to the car and no one moved in the parking lot.

They sat and listened to people yell about Ortiz. Radios in other cars. Some were listening to the same talk shows. Some had music. AC/DC. "Back in Black."

Loved them. They put them on when they went on patrol. He was always scared. Every time. But it felt good to be moving. The other guys, Peck, Long, Donaldson, singing. Rolling.

In the car, waiting, callers yelling steroids, it's over, AC/DC from the other cars in the lot.

Felt weird to be still.

They should be moving.

Shouldn't be sitting.

Moving.

He felt his breath getting fast.

"Back in Black" ended but it was Block Party Weekend so "Thunderstruck" came on and they used to listen to it when they were going out and he remembered stopping.

Being still.

Not moving.

Brain felt like it froze. Hurt.

He knew it was okay he knew he was in Boston with Artie the Sox game just got out but he had to get out even though he knew it was a Boston parking lot. He had to get out he said I'm sorry, man, and walked down the street, ran, over the highway, running, and there was a train sometimes on his right, cars stuffed with people wearing Red Sox hats and jackets and his shitty prepaid phone rang and rang and he knew it was Artie calling to ask if he was okay and he just let it ring and kept running. Artie didn't seem too mad on the ride back, said it was fine. And Artie called a few times since, like five different days, but he didn't call back. Couldn't. Too much of a pussy. The fuckin' Sox, dude, and he couldn't sit in a car with his buddy—his best friend, pretty much his only one—who bought the ticket and beers and drove him down. What the fuck.

So no city. He wished he could but the car that time told him no. He wanted to think yes. Like it was just once. But that was the start. Couldn't predict noise. He'd be on a train and hear something. See something. Lose it. Or a job.

Donaldson never called back. Frick. Months afterward. Hey, man. Nothing. Hated email but tried it. PalCorral. They never answered.

It wasn't all him. Couldn't be. They had shit going on. Wanted to forget, too. Made him sad. Yeah. Peck and Long and everyone else. Wanted to forget that they ever went. The fucking desert. All of it.

Him.

He wished he could forget himself. Get lost in something. He did. Sometimes. When he got mad, mostly. But pool. Games. The woods. Walks.

He liked the woods. Quiet there. No people except sometimes kids with dogs. The old abandoned hearse where he drank in high school. The quarry.

Around the common every day. Hurt less now, but still there. By the library.

Wished he could read better. Before he left he did a little. John Grisham, Stephen King. Tom Clancy. Those guys were great. Now he couldn't sit long enough. Mostly head down. School. Wished he could. Maybe someday. GI Bill. But no way. Not now. Hard to concentrate. Headaches. Couldn't. School, driving. Couldn't.

But he went to the library. Sports pages. Liked those better than on the computer. Box scores on screens didn't work.

They had DVDs. But it was hard to find stuff. Military history didn't work. Sports did. Even the stuff he didn't like. Notre Dame football. The fucking Yankees. So pissed he forgot he went over, he realized after. But he was starting to run low on sports. After that maybe science of the mind stuff.

His favorites before were action films, but he didn't want to try those.

He wished he liked the computer more. All the guys talked about it. Online dating. Frick talked about all the girls he met. Easy, man, Frick said. Send pictures of your junk, they come to you. Roy didn't believe it. You take dick pictures? Sure, Frick said. All the time. It works.

Frick named a few pages. PalCorral he knew. Tried to friend the guys. The others he didn't know. He looked. But he didn't want a profile. On PalCorral he didn't fit in at all. Just name and town. Roy Eggleton, Armbrister. Didn't talk about his likes. Or history.

The computer would help with jobs. If he knew where to look. He sat and tried. Made a resume. Mailed it to people. Security. Already had firearm training. Landscaping, carpentry, mill. Nothing happened. So he went to the unemployment office. Nothing for you, every time.

Before he left he thought he had it made. Auntie Blake's friend's friend, from Massachusetts. Plenty of work when you get back. Houses. Growth potential. Even in the winter. You'll be on your feet in no time. But the first houses weren't finished. They just sat there. No glass. The market, everyone said. No jobs. No home sales. No need.

So he walked. Leg hurt. When it wasn't the common or the woods it was the roads. Just go. No sidewalks. Sometimes cars got close. Walked against traffic. Wanted to see it coming. No surprises.

He walked to Wilburton a few times. Long. Twelve miles. But his leg hurt. Never went away. Doctor said it probably never would. He wanted to do Schaferville. Further. Hadn't done it yet. Fifteen, maybe longer. Before it would have been easy. But he wouldn't have walked it before. He would have driven. Now, walking. But it got dark. Maybe he'd sleep in the woods. Bring his bag and a tarp. He used to camp. Before Artie knocked up his girl and he went over. They always talked about the three Bs: baseball, beer, and boobs. Used to laugh. Camp by the river. Have a fire. Talk about Boston. The Sox. Moving there. Maybe Artie would come. Meet him somewhere. Drive out. The car there, but if he walked who cares. Carry the stuff on his back.

Wilburton wasn't bad. Their common was better. More stores. Better kept. No leaves. He thought he could do that. Rake. Sent applications. Schools. Public Works. Better than being inside all day. But no one called. He tried back. Knew he had to. They all said no openings. He wondered. Looked as much as he could. Want ads, library computers. There used to be more.

He thought about leaving. Why not? Be someplace new. Wilburton he didn't mind. Or Schaferville. Maybe Artie could get him a job. He'd been under the hood a little overseas. Remembered stuff from high school. He could learn. Good with his hands. Grateful for the opportunity. Get a place. But bills and all. Moving van. Deposit. Didn't have one now. Or last. Weekly. Schaferville had places like that. Had to. Would the garage be hot like the desert? Hoped not. It would suck in the winter. Freeze. Plastic over the windows. He'd need a hairdryer. Still cold anyway. Oil heat. Everything he did overseas and too expensive to heat a house. Maybe four good months.

There was a bar. Irish place. Did they have a pool table? Couldn't remember. Maybe. He'd go. Check it out. See how he felt.

Talk to Artie. Duh. That was it. Stop by his place. Tell him the plan. No contracting work. No security. No landscaping, janitor. Cars. Artie knew he could do it. Work hard. Study. Learn.

He could get more books. Cars. Engines. He saw that stuff. Knew it. Recognized it. The names faded. Didn't know what things were called. But he could get it back. Easy. Thinking about it made him feel good. Didn't give him a headache. Like when he thought about the contracting. Thought the whole time he had work. Got back, there was none. Just a little check. Thought he'd have it made. A porch, cable. Watch the Sox. iPhone. Grill. Instead, a check. And headaches.

Cars, though. He could do that.

Rather be outside. In the sun. But garage doors opened. Cold in the winter. Probably better than his apartment.

Hoped Schaferville had pool. If not he'd have to walk in for games. Just for fun instead of money. But he could get a bike. That would work. Exercise. Stay in shape. Look good. Start a real profile. With pictures. Wait for them to come. Could it be that easy? Frick was full of shit. Had to be. But the way he talked. There was something in it. Wasn't all lies.

Or maybe get a car. Boston was a one-time thing. It would be okay. Get a job, settle in. Not worry so much. Move away from it, no headaches. News on the radio. Lose himself in his new thing. Be okay to drive.

He walked behind the L'il Bee to the woods entrance. School day. Didn't like to go in after. Kids. He remembered cutting school. Going out there. The hearse. The quarry. Crushed cans. Rick Robards worked at the grocery store. For twenty bucks he'd leave a twelver on the loading dock. Expensive. But beer. Artie wanted to save the cans. Return them. Sixty fuckin' cents. Where were you supposed to return beer cans? Small town. Crush them. Keep drinking.

Beginning of the summer. Couldn't remember the exact year. The quarry. Artie brought his girl out there. Heat lightning. Thought they'd get electrocuted. A sign or something. Carrying the twelve-pack so Artie could hold hands with his girl. They were okay. Not too cute. Thank God. He saw dudes and their girls at school. Tough dudes, like voc, cars, mushy. Wearing Slayer shirts, being pussies. Artie never did that. His girl Christa was okay. She could drink. Finished her four quick. Before him. Before Artie. Belched like a man.

Heat lightning flickered. Granite peaks named in spray-paint. Tall one was "Tits." Made no sense. Should have been "Dick," maybe. Two peaks? Tits. But no pairs. Just singles. Granite. Sharp on the edges. People wore shoes in. Too sharp not to. Hurt less when you hit.

Artie couldn't swim. And girls didn't jump. One did once. What was her name? Got fucked up. Rocks. Hit her head. Wore all black now. Walked every day. Like him.

He jumped. That night. Heat lightning, four beers. Never did it before. Could swim okay. Learned when he was little. Didn't know he was going to. Just stood up, pulled off his shirt, jeans.

Socks, shoes. I'm doing it, he said. Christa said no, Roy, wait. Wait a minute. It's dark. They heard splashes. People jumping. Don't. You'll get hurt.

He walked toward Tits. Artie said wait, man, do a small one first. Do Cunt. But it was like he wasn't in his head. Like in the tent. Someone else. His body moving and he could see it even though it was dark. Watching. Like he was dead. He walked to Tits and stood on the lip. They were right. It was sharp. Bloody feet later. All the feet that had jumped off and still sharp.

Felt like a long time before he hit. In the air for days. But just a second.

It hurt. Knew why people wore shoes. Only for a few seconds but it hurt.

He was in. Or was he? Cold. Tasted like dirt. He thought he was swimming up but it was cold and dark and tasted like dirt. Maybe this was what it was like to be dead. Maybe he was. Maybe they buried him.

Nothing under his feet. Swimming up. Or not. Dirt taste. Dead. Then his head broke. He was up.

The path back took ten minutes. Water still like dirt in his mouth. Hard to see but he heard voices and heat lightning lit everything. He got back and they said how was it? Awesome he said and did it again. They didn't tell him not to anymore.

5.

I went to the cafeteria at lunchtime. The nerd table gave me like twenty bucks! I sat right down with them and said hey, I hope you guys can help me out. My mom needs some medicine. She's really sick. And they knew I was kidding but they gave me the money anyway.

* * *

I just listened back. I forgot to go to the library to see how much football players make.

* * *

Ross came home early today.

He said I hear you've been hanging out with Ding.

I wanted to say only for more than a year. Then I wanted to say I went looking for him yesterday but couldn't find him. But I didn't. Instead I said yeah.

He goes cut the shit.

When I asked why he said Ding's been to jail.

Here's what we said:

So what?

You think it's good to hang out with someone who's been to jail?

I don't care.

Think of how it looks.

I was like how'd you hear, anyway? and he said I have my ways.

So I was all like whatever and he went no, seriously, think of how it looks if my sister is hanging with a guy like that.

I said I barely even see him.

Just when you do your business, right? I heard about you and your business.

So I was all like fuck you, Ross.

He goes seriously, that guy is bad news.

I left.

I don't know what Ross's deal is.

Tomorrow I'm gonna find Ding and get rid of that iPod.

* * *

I remembered to go to the library today. There were so many nerds. Tietz was there and he turned white when I walked by.

Those quarterbacks make a lot of money. Wide receivers and running backs, too. There are a few defense guys who make some loot—that's the position he plays, defense. Five million, ten million.

* * *

On the way home I saw Ding's car parked in front of the L'il Bee. I said gonna be here in fifteen minutes? and he said I can be. I told him I had something for him at the house.

Don was passed out on the couch when I got home. I went in, got the iPod and the watch and went back.

When I got there he was like wanna go for a ride?

I said where?

Nowhere.

I got in. We drove past the school. The football team was practicing in the field.

He said got something for me?

I took out the iPod and the watch.

He said I don't know how you get all this stuff.

He totally knows. He just pretends he doesn't.

He always asks what I want, even though he knows I'm done with that fireworks shit. But it's way cheaper for him to give me a few M-80s every time, so I can't blame him for trying.

He tried giving me M-80s and Silver Salutes. I said no, cash.

We drove around for a while. Neither of us said anything. I like that. Being quiet. If I ever go out with anyone it'll be like that. I don't want to have to talk all the time. All those girls at school, always telling their girlfriends everything about their boyfriends. It's like, why do you have to talk all the time? About everything? But driving around quiet, I like that.

Fifty, he said. For both.

He usually goes forty on an iPod.

I said you can go higher.

He tried throwing in some M-80s.

I told him no.

He said no one wants watches right now. And iPods aren't as big as they used to be.

I said fine, pull over.

He stopped on this stretch of road that was all trees and put his hazards on. I felt like we'd stopped in that exact spot before, maybe a few times.

I pulled up my shirt and pulled down my bra. He looked at me with these big eyes the way he does. He never comes right out and says it. Always has to bargain. And every time he tries to put his hands on them, and every time I'm like yeah, right, asshole and pull my shirt down. He can look all he wants as long as he pays big, but he can't touch. I'll give him another bloody nose.

I'll take you back, he said.

So we drove back and didn't talk. He pulled around the L'il Bee dumpster and pulled out a wad of bills. He counted out four twenties.

For the iPod, the watch, and something extra, he said. Always like that: something extra. He said you know you could get more. And I was like do you want me to kick your ass again?

He said you want those M-80s? I was like sure.

He got out. I saw the trunk pop open in the rearview. He came back with a brown bag. Maybe Mom made it at the mill.

He said see if you can get a laptop. Or one of those pad computers.

I said see ya and got out of the car.

* * *

I went to the library again today. Nerd city.

Anyway, I'm fucked.

I've got eight hundred dollars. Concord is like seven hundred a month. Manchester is about the same. And they need first, last, and security. That's a ton of money. Then I need to buy food and stuff.

Unless I get a job I'm stuck, even if I do find a bunch of laptops.

* * *

I'm at the development, down in the basement of one of those houses. It's a few down from where I was last time. This is the first one I could find that was open.

Cold in here. There's plastic over where the windows would be. It doesn't help.

This is a Silver Salute. After this I only have two left, then the bag of M-80s Ding gave me yesterday.

I won't miss this at all. I need money.

I'm gonna put it on the basement floor. Here goes:

(sound of explosion)

That was fucking LOUD.

Let's see.

Nah, the floor still looks the same.

Okay, now the M-80. Different place this time.

Here we go!

(sound of explosion)

AWESOME.

I thought maybe there would be a crater. There isn't, but there's something. Burn marks.

* * *

I wonder what demolition is like. Get a bunch of explosives and figure out which ones would blow shit up the best. That would be a cool job.

* * *

I forgot to talk about school.

I failed another test. Geometry. Maybe I should've stuck with nursing. But anatomy is harder than geometry.

Trombley says it's early enough in the semester so I can still pass, but I'll have to apply myself.

That's what teachers always say. But no matter what happens, I wind up in the next year. So whatever.

* * *

The first place I should go is the L'il Bee. But I don't want to because of Mom. No way do I wanna work with her. Even if I am getting paid for it.

Same thing with the mill. So I guess it's restaurants.

* * *

At school today I went outside to the corner where all the voc kids hang out.

I told all those guys I have M-80s and Silver Salutes. I thought I'd sell them. But no one wanted any.

One guy was like that's kid's stuff. Where were you when I needed you in sixth grade?

Everyone laughed.

I almost went to the nerd table inside. But those guys are all afraid of me. I'm surprised no one's ever ratted me out. If one of those dumb shits lost a finger or an eye because I sold 'em an M-80 I'd be fucked. So forget it.

* * *

I'll go back to the library tomorrow and find out how to apply for jobs. Then after school I'll come home and change and go around.

6.

Zachariah Tietz wrote game shows.

Portions of them, anyway. He'd filled two notebooks with ideas for challenges. But before *Love Balloon*, he'd never been able to visualize a show from start to finish. The individual segments in his notebooks, he realized, were standalones. Trying to get them to work together felt forced—when the shows made it to television, he would see their seams grinding against each other. If he was going to be a good game show producer there couldn't be any seams.

With *Love Balloon*, his ideas came together.

Almost.

Zachariah had never seen or heard of a show that was completed over two seasons—that is, a game show where the end of the first season was the halfway point. *Love Balloon* would be the first. The success of his first televised show would get him out of Armbrister—and out of the voc wing—forever. He'd move to whatever neighborhood in Hollywood housed successful game show producers. For Christmas (and maybe Thanksgiving) he'd visit his dad in a limo. Everyone in Armbrister would know his story: son of a single millworker finds Hollywood success.

The problem with his show was the second season. He had no idea what to plan for the challenges and speed rounds after the end of the first half—the bachelors and their competitions were no problem. But how could he know what to do after the balloon? In the apartment? Viewers needed some kind of structure to rely on, but he hadn't figured out what that structure was.

I hope I can figure out the second season, he thought.

He sat for a minute, waiting to see if anything felt different. Nothing did.

That was good, right? When the bleachers had been fit to collapse he hadn't had any sort of tingle: the pass was picked off—that was all.

* * *

Lunchtime was the worst.

He wished he could eat in the library. Ms. Collmenter and Ms. Petrie, though, rigidly enforced a no food or drink rule, especially in the computer area. He might get away with the Library Lunch Challenge, but at some point they'd catch him and maybe revoke his library privileges. So, his choices were the single-stall handicapped bathroom in the hallway or on the walk to the library. The latter was worse. Last year he started eating rapidly while walking as slowly as possible. No one noticed. Since his weight gain, though, anything involving food gained a negative charge: *Hey, Zits, you're so hungry you have to eat while you walk? There's a room for that! Or are you eating on the way to the cafeteria to eat?*

He preferred the handicapped bathroom, but for the past few days Jamie Townes, the wheelchair girl, would be in there at the start of the lunch period. When she came out, fifteen minutes into the twenty-five minute lunch break, the bathroom stunk so bad he couldn't enter.

Skipping lunch altogether in favor of going to the library would be easiest, but he couldn't bring himself to do it. Not eating made him feel woozy. The last thing he needed was more trouble with math and measurements.

When the lunch bell rang, he went straight outside. There had to be someplace where he could eat his sandwich in seclusion before heading to the library.

The only spot he could see was a clump of bushes at the far end of the football field, where older kids smoked and made out.

The cafeteria was out. Sitting by himself was an invitation for trouble.

Until last year lunch was never a problem. He sat with his soccer friends Rick and Jim and Kenny and Sal. But following his accident, a stream of kids arrived at the table to make fun of him—and, then, him and them—and his friends moved away. First they talked to him less, then not at all.

He assumed things would go back to normal after a few days and discovered, as days turned to weeks, that the new normal was that his friends had moved to different tables and gave icy, minimal responses to his questions.

The summer would make everything better, he had thought. When he got back, he'd start playing soccer again and things would be the way they were. He'd practice through July and August and make a goal the first game back, shut everyone up, and go on eating lunch with his friends like nothing happened.

Instead he gained his weight.

Everything that happened in the wake of his accident was just a taste. There were kids at the high school who hadn't heard about it, but his size was obvious to all. He supposed he could join the Fat Table, but he'd seen the way people gravitated to it for the express purpose of picking on those kids. Besides, sitting there would be an admission. He'd gained some weight over the summer was all. Like the doctor said, it happened. Puberty. He'd grow, and the weight would distribute itself evenly.

If the handicapped bathroom was full he didn't know what he'd do.

I hope no one is in there.

He walked down the hall as fast as he could, feeling his belly and breasts jiggling rhythmically. He was still sometimes shocked by the way his new body felt and moved.

The door was unlocked.

Later, Zachariah thought back and realized he had willed the bathroom empty without meaning to. Just like he had kept the bleachers from collapsing.

* * *

In the library, he researched game shows.

The broken ones interested him the most.

He knew *Press Your Luck* from reruns. Contestants answered questions to gain turns at a big board, where they pushed a button to land a fast-moving frame over cash or prizes. If a contestant's frame landed on a "Whammy"—a cartoon that made fun of you—all cash and prizes disappeared.

Some guy who had watched hundreds of taped episodes made it to the bonus round. Most people who made it to the big board only stayed for a few minutes before they hit a Whammy. But this guy had discovered that the frame moved in a pattern. After a few tries to get the timing right, every turn yielded more money or spins or both. He was on for so long that the show had to keep taping his final round on the next day. The producers were mad, but what could they do? He hadn't broken any rules—he was smart enough to recognize a pattern.

Zachariah didn't want *Love Balloon* to be beatable. Most of the time, dating shows favored guys who looked like underwear models: they were handsome and strong and basically had everything going for themselves. They didn't need to win anything because they had already won. None of them ever had to sit in a stinky bathroom stall to eat another peanut butter sandwich at lunch. They had moms. Their monogrammed backpacks didn't draw jeers. When they played soccer they scored goals. They didn't have dads who drank too much and got mad at nothing. They talked to girls and got jobs and left their hometowns to live in New York or Boston.

They knew the pattern.

But there were other people on the shows. Normal-looking people, sometimes even fat ones. Like the guy who figured out *Press Your Luck*. He looked crazy.

Zachariah had watched the few heavy people on game shows more closely since he gained his weight. When they won they were happier than their skinny counterparts, and when they lost they didn't look bothered. They were already used to losing all the time.

That was a pattern, too.

He wondered if their lives were like his. Maybe they grew up with dads who thought they were going somewhere but got stuck working in a mill putting coffee trays into boxes. There was nothing to do but drink can after can of Venerable and watch sports on TV after work, either at home or in a bar. Sports reminded his dad of high school and Armbrister's state championship. Zachariah knew his dad told everyone about playing football. But he'd work in the mill forever. Partially because he, Zachariah, had come along.

When he rode his bike around town Zachariah saw kids hanging around who he recognized from the junior high halls. Kids who once played soccer or football, now smoking cigarettes in front of the L'il Bee. They were only a few years older than him, but had creased faces like his dad's.

Recipes had patterns, too. He was horrible at math, but he understood how food worked. Bread, especially. And pastry. Pasta dough. Mrs. Lafrancoise always shook her head when she watched him bake. Zachariah, she'd say, you have a gift. She was the one who convinced him to enroll in voc.

All the kids who wore denim jackets and T-shirts bearing the names of scary-sounding bands did voc. They drove noisy cars and drank beer. Even before his soccer accident, before his weight, he didn't want to hang around with that crowd—taking regular classes would make more sense (except maybe math). But Mrs. Lafrancoise told him that because of the way he knew about bread—just knew, she said—he would have no problem getting a job at a nice restaurant. He could be a pastry chef. Or a baker. And because he came from a low-income family, he might be eligible for a scholarship to a culinary school.

* * *

Zachariah heard the TV as he opened the door.

Uh-oh.

When his dad came home early it wasn't because something good happened. Which meant he had already started drinking. And a beating, probably, unless he escaped.

The TV was loud with some kind of car race. Zachariah, still holding the screen door handle, turned and began to tiptoe back out of the house.

He could walk back to the school library, open until five. Or he could walk downtown to the Double Scoop, although doing so would probably mean getting picked on. He missed sitting at its dark wood tables, a dish of ice cream in front of him, working on a game show. Since his weight gain, the rewards the place offered—quiet music, sun pouring through the windows—were not worth the inevitability of kids walking by his table, saying that fatties didn't need more ice cream. But that risk far outweighed the sock of tennis balls in his father's closet.

"I HEAR YOU!"

Oh no.

Paul Tietz appeared in the kitchen doorway, eyes red and bleary, holding a can of Venerable. His short-sleeved work shirt was unbuttoned low, a stained white tee poking out from underneath.

"Trying to get out without me hearin' you, huh?"

Zachariah said nothing.

"What did you learn in school today?"

If he said "nothing," his father would deride him for being stupid. If he mentioned something he learned, his dad would accuse him of trying to outsmart his old man.

"What are you watching?"

"Some car race," he said. "Who cares? Why would I want to watch a bunch of guys drive in circles? Going nowhere."

Zachariah nodded.

"What's for dinner?"

Zachariah wanted to tell his father it was two-thirty in the afternoon.

"You're always thinking about it. You're probably thinking about food right now."

Zachariah said nothing.

"I SAID WHAT'S FOR DINNER?"

Before he knew it Zachariah was on the floor. A sunburst of pain blossomed in one kidney, fresh and raw. He hollered.

"ANSWER ME!"

Zachariah moved his mouth to form words. None came.

A fresh blossom on the other side.

Still no words, but a howl.

"WHAT'S FOR DINNER?"

"Ah," Zachariah said.

His father stood over him.

"Ah . . . I'll make . . . Ruh . . . Ravioli."

It was Paul's favorite. There was always frozen hamburger in the freezer.

"I'm hungry," Paul said and stomped back to the living room.

7.

LIBRARY. CAR BOOKS WERE GOOD. PICTURES. Understood more every day. Remembered.

The recruiter said easier to get work when you come home. You gain stature. College if you want. GI Bill. Grants. But their looks when he went into the job place. Like here we go again. No. Couldn't be because there were none. It was him. The way he looked. Talked. Something. So he'd learn up. Go see Artie. Say hey, man. I haven't called because I've been studying.

Pictures. Helped him remember. Under the hood. With Peck. Gotta be cold, Peck said overseas. Make sure. Sounds easy. It isn't. Guys hurt themselves. Everything Peck said was like that. Stuff he didn't know that he should've. Common sense. Maybe because he had none. He thought back. School. What an asshole. Making excuses. Trying to get off. That got beat out of him. Basic. He learned fast. Talking himself out of it. Not to make excuses, sir, but I thought this was clean enough. Then McSorley that friggin' prick put him on toilets for a week. Maybe having your face in shit will make you realize there's no such thing as clean enough, private. There's clean and not clean and you'll learn which is which by putting your face in both. After that McSorley gave it to him for weeks. Called him a slacker. But he didn't ever fuck up again. At least not in basic. The guys said you can't talk to him like that. I know, I know. A week of your corn and peas. Trust me. They laughed.

After the library he walked. Every day around the common. Exercise. To get his leg back to where it was. And to get out of the apartment. Okay most of the day. When the wind blew he could feel it. Stuffed up the cracks with towels. Plastic over windows. Didn't matter. Wasn't cold like on his skin. Inside him, his bones. Never got warm. Not even winter yet. The library was always hot. One reason he went.

The same people on the common. Not the same time every day. Checked the church clock. Lots of dog people. Guy with husky. Tillie Tompkins. Her yappy dog. Went to the same church Auntie Blake did. Hello, he said. Being polite. Making an effort. She looked at him the first time and said oh my. Her face. Made him remember going to Boston for field trips. Zoos. Animals knew they were being watched. Couldn't change it. Tried not to care. Same as on patrol. Villagers watching. Saying hello. Saw it in her eyes. He still tried. Her and the dog both. She didn't mean anything by it. But still.

Across the common he saw that girl. From the quarry. High school. Always wearing black. What was her name? He hadn't been there. Artie's friend Gil said he knew someone who was. Like a melon hitting pavement, he said. They pulled her out. Didn't know why he cared so much. She jumped. Maybe that was all. So did he. Like someone else was pulling the strings. Maybe she felt the same before her head hit.

Remembered that same summer. They went back to the quarry. After he jumped. Artie and Christa. Some of her friends. Dudes.

He thought that was weird. Artie didn't mind. Couldn't remember their names. Knew faces.

Two twelvers. Roy carried one again so they could hold hands. The other guys were like you're the man, dude. We heard you did Tits your first night. Yeah, he said. That shit is hard. Gonna do it again? He sat there by the fire. I don't know, maybe. Drank. Listened to stories. Waited. Like it was gonna happen again. It didn't. Drank four. Knew he was ripping someone off. Three each. Didn't care. Those guys talking about it. How tough he was. He wanted to.

Didn't even stand up. Wouldn't walk to the ledge. Nothing.

They called Roy a pussy. Artie was like all right, lay off. No one else would do it. I'm not your bitch, he said. You fucking do it. No one would. They shut up. But he still felt it. They passed him in the halls. Had looks.

When he signed up he thought about that. Coming back would take away the looks. But it didn't. The college ones shook their heads. Asked if he was going to fight for oil. He got mad. Some skinny kid in glasses and a sweater. Punched him. First fight in a long time. Didn't matter. Artie's friends still looked at him. Because of the quarry. He wouldn't jump. Didn't matter he was going.

That girl, all in black, across the common. He wanted to talk to her. Say I walk, too. Be nice to talk to someone. Even if they didn't. Just be there. But she was all the way across. Couldn't cut it. Had to play it cool. Like he didn't care. That was better. Not sure why. Just was. He watched her walk around and down toward her house. He didn't think she'd lived there before. Maybe she did. Her place now. Everyone knew. Artie told him. Old van in the yard. Colored paper in the windows.

He knew the type. From school. Skinny. Wore big black glasses. Wrote in notebooks at lunch but called them journals.

Listened to fucked up music. Not like radio stuff. But he didn't remember her. They all looked the same. Were smarter. Talked about stuff he didn't understand. Didn't like sports. He remembered that. Right? All black? Always. Summer, winter. Didn't matter. Sometimes an umbrella. No dog. Just a walk. Fucked up when her head hit. Changed.

Still saw kids like that at the library. Writing in their journals. Reading their books. He just read box scores and car books. Foreign and domestic. Which did Artie do? He'd check. If domestic, maybe Artie knew someone. A network. Had to be like that. In basic they thought it was like that. Yeah, Peck always said. When we get back the shit is gonna be awesome. Come down to Bama and we'll grill steaks. Get wasted. Go to a game. Every year. Bring our kids. Check out each other's wives. He always said that. About the wives. They all laughed. Every time. He meant everyone would check out his. Peck, he knew. And they would. Bring your buddies. Their wives. Check them out, too. Friend of yours, friend of mine. Every year. Get to know some people. Good people. Help each other out. Thought he'd bring Artie. Christa. Talk about hunting, cars, football. Artie was a hunter. Went out every year. Looking for deer. Got a couple. Artie didn't mention hunting since he got back. He usually just talked about that stuff. Probably didn't because of what happened. He understood. Never much for it. Had a rifle, though. Artie gave it to him in high school. They went out once. Fucking boring. Like being overseas. Sat in a blind and waited. Deer never came. In Maine. Some family friend's cabin. Great place. Drank a lot. Dirty cards. Said he'd go again. Cabin got sold.

Common every day, but woods some. Yesterday he got up early. Nightmare. Headache behind his eyes. Someone chasing him.

Didn't know who. Or what. Sometimes tanks. Trucks. Dudes with guns. Couldn't remember. Always being chased. Tried going back to sleep. Couldn't. Went for a walk. L'il Bee parking lot full of cars. People buying coffee before work. No one in the woods. Too early. Ten minutes in he couldn't hear cars. Air cold and damp. But different than in his apartment. A morning thing he remembered.

He heard a crackle. A deer walked out. Huge. Stood there long enough to count points. Eight.

Woods were posted. That was why. Signs on trees when he did walks. To the hearse, the quarry. He wondered if Tits was still sharp. Probably. Granite was strong.

Roads during the day. Schaferville was far. At first thought he could get there and back easy. It was hard. Hilly. Both ways. Hurt his leg. And traffic. No sidewalk. Small shoulder. Cars hauling ass.

After the woods yesterday and the common today he started walking it and couldn't finish. Hurt too much.

He went home. Got the mail. Never anything good. The *Armbrister Sentinel*, a bunch of official-looking stuff. From the army. No check. Another ten days. Knew those envelopes. Kept the rest in a pile on the table.

He liked the paper okay. Wasn't the *Globe* or the *Herald*. Big print. Easy. Short articles. About the football team. Good players. This one defensive back. Scholarship, probably, the paper said. Not Durham or Plymouth or Keene. A real school. Division I.

He'd go see the one good defensive back. Keep walking. At night, pool. Dry lately. Only a few games a night. Lefty all the time. Kept him from getting bored. Sox sucked. Everyone hurt.

8.

Today at the library I found some blank resumes online. I filled one in. There's not much on there. I mean, I go to school. I tried soccer for a while. That's it. I can't tell them about M-80s or anything like that.

* * *

It would've taken me all day to walk to the part of town where the restaurants are. I forgot about that until it was time to go. So I borrowed a bike from the rack outside after ninth period. Just a few steps from my locker to the door, then a few more to the rack. That old security guard is only there when everyone comes in and after tenth period. Nice and easy.

I brought the nicest clothes I had in a paper bag and changed in the bathroom. I hope no one saw me in that dorky outfit.

There are no sidewalks, so I felt the cars whiz by.

At each place I said hello, I'm looking for employment. They all said would you like to fill out an application? And I said I brought a resume. Ten copies. I didn't think I was going to use them all, but I did. A few of those places looked at me like I knew what I was doing. It's cool.

* * *

This morning when I was having cereal with Ross, Don said where the hell did that bike come from? I was like what bike? Don said you know damn well what bike. I thought it'd be worse if I lied so I was like well, I borrowed it from a kid I know, which is kinda true. I mean, I didn't know who I borrowed it from, but I was gonna return it. But Don said you stole it, you little shit.

I started laughing because of what he said, little shit.

He goes you think it's funny? You think it's funny to steal and then laugh in my face about it? I'll show you funny. And then he slapped me. First time since he got back.

Ross kept eating.

It mostly stung.

Don said your mother might not give a shit about the way you act, but I'm not gonna live under the safe roof as a disrespecting thief.

I could feel his handprint across my face.

I said I borrowed it.

He goes so now you're a liar, too. Want another one?

I said I'm going to return it right now.

You get your act together, he said. Cut the shit. There are more important things to think about than yourself, you know. You think about this family.

I wanted to say this isn't your family, but I didn't want to get hit again.

No one said anything when I put the bike back on the rack.

It was gone after school.

* * *

Those fucking nerds were sitting at their table today at lunch. I went over and was like hey, you know, my mom needs more medicine, she's not feeling very well. One of them said we gave you money already. I said she's very sick, and she appreciates donations.

Nobody moved, so I was like I heard she has some space in her room. Like, an extra hospital bed. In case anyone needs it.

They all kept looking at me, so I was like in case anyone here needs it.

They put money on the table.

Easy.

* * *

I went to the quarry after school. Steve and all those guys were up there. I thought they might be.

Mary was there. And Earl, jumping.

Steve said Dixon.

I said what's up?

Earl had a towel. I pointed at it. He nodded.

Steve said big game this weekend.

I went that's what I hear.

He asked if I was gonna go. I told him I was thinking about it.

He said why don't you come with us?

I looked at Mary. She nodded.

I said I'd go with them.

He asked if I knew Whispering Pines. I said yeah. He said we'll meet over there and get fucked up and then go to the game. You in?

When I asked when to meet, he said dusk. Best time.

I asked if that would leave us enough time to walk over. Earl laughed and said how old are you, anyway?

I said what do you mean? Steve said you don't have your license yet?

I shook my head.

Mary was still smiling.

Steve said we'll have plenty of time to get over there. Don't worry.

I said cool. I'll be here at dusk.

Steve asked if I wanted a beer. Mary was drinking one. I said yeah. He threw one to me just like last time.

I opened it and he went what's new with you?

I said nothing. Looking for work.

Earl said where you been lookin'? I told him restaurant row. He said you might get something over there. Those places go through a lot of people. Jobs suck. But hey, they're jobs. Got any experience?

I shook my head and took a swig.

Steve said try the mills?

I said nope. Don't want to block Earl.

Earl said haha. Then, good money over there.

I said I'll never get in. Everyone in town wants to.

Mary finished her beer. I watched her crush the can and throw it toward the quarry.

Just dumb luck, he said. Like, they need someone, see your application, boom.

I said it's not that easy.

He said no reason for it. Just dumb luck. Seriously. Boom.

* * *

Don's not here. Neither is Mom. Or Ross. I'm in the kitchen. Mom bought bananas. Or Don did.

We never have bananas.

* * *

Hey. Everyone just came in.

* * *

They visited some recruiter.

Mom cooked a chicken. It started smelling really good.

She came by and knocked on the door and said are you in there? I said yeah. She said come eat.

I went out there and she had a candle on the table. She never does that. She said we're gonna eat as a family. I can't remember the last time we were all home at the same time.

She made the chicken, and green beans.

We sat down and she said Ross, tell your sister about today.

He told me they talked to Nebraska. It's his first choice. Pretty soon he'd sign a letter of intent.

I said awesome. I don't know anything about that school. Or that state. I think there's corn.

Great school, Don said. Great football school.

Then he said you'd think maybe your sister would want to see you play.

She is, he said. With Steve Remlinger and Earl Lang.

I didn't even know Earl's last name.

Mom said who are they? and Ross said Steve used to go to Armbrister High. Before he dropped out.

I told Ross to shut up. What an asshole, right? Why would he do that?

Don put both hands on the table and stood up and said are they the ones who convinced you to steal the bike?

I was like I told you, I borrowed it. And I gave it back! Then, of course, Mom was like what bike? Don started telling her about finding it out back. Mom was all oh, Dixon, like she always is when she's mad. I said I told you, I borrowed it. Don said bullshit. You're turning into a thief and I think it's because of those guys you're hanging around with.

I said I don't hang out with them too much and Ross said except for when you go to the quarry. I was like Ross, shut up and Don slapped me. Same place as last time.

He said it's time you learned some respect.

Mom said Don's right. You never used to be like this.

I said like what? And Mom said a thief. Hanging around with the wrong crowd. I said I never hung out with any crowd and she said well, you're with the wrong one now.

I've known those guys for a while, at least a little. So I said whatever.

Don got up and said don't talk to your mother like that and I was like whatever, again. So he goes you need to get your act together. I was like you're on the couch drunk every day, you should talk. He started yelling and Mom started crying and Ross just sat there.

I ran out. Don stood at the door and yelled YOU GET YOUR ASS BACK HERE! I could see people looking out their windows at us.

I didn't know where to go, so I went to the parking lot.

Ding was sitting in his car.

I got in.

He said got something for me?

I shook my head.

He asked if I was okay.

I nodded. Probably looked like shit. I said where are you going?

He said nowhere. Then he handed me a bottle. Want some of this?

I took it and pulled. Jesus. Whiskey. Made me cough. He laughed when I gave it back. Not a whiskey girl, huh?

I said no. Venerable. Then I asked him to pass the whiskey back.

He did. I took another pull.

He went how old are you again? I said not old enough for you. Then I told him to take me for a ride. I started to lift my shirt and he said not here.

He backed out of the parking lot and turned the radio on. Block Party Weekend is all week now, I guess. Van Halen.

He turned and I knew when he did we were going to the Pines. There's nothing else out that way. He pulled in and said do you know this place? and I said yeah except I think it came out weird. Like there was still crying caught in my throat or something.

He pulled into the driveway of one of the houses I use and lit a smoke. He held out the pack and I took one. Then he gave me his lighter.

So, he said.

I said so back.

He took a big drag off his cigarette and held it. The smoke came out of his nose. Cool-looking.

When he finished he opened his window and flicked it out. There's always butts and glass out there.

He said this is a good place to get away from everyone. They're never gonna finish these.

I was like yeah. Thinking of that cigarette butt. Everyone trying to get away but there's no place to go so we all wind up out there. Ding in his car asking me questions he already knows the answers to. Steve and Earl before games. Everyone goes to the Pines. Smoking butts and drinking. Except my stupid brother.

9.

ZACHARIAH ATE IN SILENCE IN THE handicapped bathroom.

A pee welled in his bladder. His last few had been flecked with blood, and the dull ache he had grown accustomed to after Paul hit him was worse than usual.

It hadn't occurred to him until he woke that he should've used his powers to stop him. He'd forgotten. Stupid.

He wanted to go to the nurse for some aspirin or Advil—his dad must've finished the bottle—but she'd ask questions he couldn't answer. If anyone found out about the beatings, there would be more waiting for him. And if he was taken from his dad, he'd land in a group home, which would be worse than getting hit a little—the residents would pick on him and beat him up and maybe even rape him. Zachariah heard that happened sometimes. Plus, the food was probably terrible.

So he finished his sandwich and went back to the library.

He'd forgotten to pack his game show notebook and wasn't in the mood for research. He'd look at recipes.

None of the measurements made sense to him. In class, he always had trouble with conversions—there were so many to remember!—and he sometimes failed his food math tests. Mrs.

Lafrancoise was always nice about it, saying he had other gifts. And when he had to double or triple recipes, he always did so without measuring; the dishes came out right. No math required. He just knew.

He looked online at recipes featuring ingredients he had never used. He imagined what it would be like to prepare arugula, mahimahi, pork tenderloin. When *Love Balloon* got big he'd have dinner parties for all of his famous friends and make dishes with these new ingredients.

Being famous would be fun. People would say there goes Zack Fox, the greatest game show writer of all time instead of there goes that loser Zachariah Tietz.

It was soccer that did it. He played in a rec league on fall weekends, so he was pretty good. Not great, but not so terrible that he embarrassed himself either. Maybe a little rusty that day. He liked playing defense the best. It wasn't loud, popular guys who played that position—those kids, who he thought looked like underwear models, were always strikers, hitting their chests and yelling when they scored goals. Zachariah preferred to quietly keep the other team's chest-thumpers from scoring, taking immense satisfaction in breaking up drives to the net. His friend Rick was a striker. He wasn't very good, though. Usually Jim and Sal played midfield, and Kenny was goalie.

Out on the field during lunch, a few weeks before they were let out for the summer, he assumed his usual spot by the goal and waited for play to come to him.

Rick was the only one of his friends playing. Malvern O'Hare, an eighth grader who played with the high school kids on the Armbrister traveling team, got the ball and moved toward Zachariah and the goal. The other kids playing defense were out of position.

Malvern's feints and dekes didn't work on Zachariah, who focused on the opposing player's torso rather than his feet. When the ball spun up from the ground Zachariah jumped to bounce it off his chest. The spin, though, altered the ball's trajectory. He was hit in the nuts.

Zachariah was first startled, then relieved that he hadn't been hit harder. The ball's spin had prevented him from being hurt. That could have been really bad, he remembered thinking in midair—milliseconds before Malvern O'Hare's sneakered foot connected squarely with his nuts.

The number of people who claimed to have witnessed what happened next grew over summer break. Zachariah, having been dragged to every Armbrister football game since his mother left when he was three, was familiar with this phenomenon; he knew that not everyone who claimed to be present when Roger Conroy threw The Pass had been there, just as he knew that no one watched pickup soccer games during lunch. The only people involved were the ones playing; everyone else was busy doing something on their own or in groups. Yet the whispered—and sometimes shouted—claims of having seen Zachariah Tietz simultaneously piss himself and puke during lunch that day grew by the hour afterward, until everyone who claimed to be present would have overflowed Armbrister Middle's auditorium.

Zachariah felt his pants dampen as he lay on the ground, gasping for breath in the seconds before brutal nausea wrenched his stomach with more force than he knew was possible. This is the hardest I have ever been hit in the nuts, he thought. He'd been hit above the waist enough to know what to expect, but never so hard below that the contents of his stomach evacuated themselves on their own accord. He was shocked by the speed and thrust of first his lunch, then his breakfast as he struggled to his knees, hands on the ground—so shocked that he did not immediately think of the consequences of his accident, just the pain.

Malvern O'Hare, returning from depositing the ball from the net, stood over Zachariah.

"Oh, man," he said. "I'm really—"

Zachariah puked again.

Malvern didn't ogle as Zachariah heaved onto the field grass. He is given credit, though, for noticing the spreading darkness on Zachariah's cords.

"Look!" he shouted, wonder in his voice. "He's puking and pissing!"

Zachariah's instinct was to flee, but he was again incapacitated by vomiting.

The spectacular nature of the accident dictated there was no exit strategy. Any chance that he might somehow leave with his predicament unnoticed was dashed by Malvern's amazed cry, drawing a crowd of curiosity seekers from an adjacent field.

The first bell rang. Zachariah, still heaving, looked up to find a small throng around him.

He wiped vomit residue from his mouth. The pain in his nuts felt like a new heart, pumping sickness to every part of his body.

Malvern O'Hare tried—and failed—to pull on a serious face. "I'm sorry I kicked you, mate," he said, smirking. "It was an accident."

Zachariah nodded weakly.

"I never saw anyone puke and piss themselves before."

Zachariah didn't know how to respond to this. Neither had he.

Rick stood, hands on his hips, watching.

"Rick," Zachariah said. Even speaking was an effort. He wanted to lie down. "I—"

From across the field, Mr. Danforth, the leather-lunged shop teacher, yelled "FIRST BELL," which translated to: you're going to be late.

Rick turned and, without looking back, walked toward the door.

The gawking ring slowly broke up. Zachariah struggled to rise, feeling upon himself the pressure of dozens of pairs of eyes from craning heads. He waited to get used to the pain, but every second remained agonizing, as if new. Presently his nuts began to thud. Each now weighed at least half a ton.

He couldn't go back inside. His cords were dripping with piss, and his shirt bore jets of smelly, hardening puke. And there was still the matter of his throbbing nuts. There was no way he could concentrate on anything. He had to go home.

He found walking possible at a greatly reduced pace. Zachariah cut slowly around the building and started back for his house. If any teacher asked what he was doing, there was ample evidence that he needed to change on his shirt and dripping from his pants. But, somehow, no one saw him.

It took twice as long to get home as usual. Several times he had to stop and sit down. At first he thought the pain might have diminished since he was kicked, but walking back—movement—meant new, never before experienced dimensions of nausea gripping his stomach, his nuts, pumping through his body.

Cars honked as he lumbered down the sidewalk.

He soaked his cords and shirt in warm water and vinegar when he got home. While he showered, he thought about Rick, standing there with his hands on his hips. How he had seen Zachariah on the ground and had walked away.

Maybe he didn't want to be late, Zachariah thought. He was worried about getting to class.

But he knew this wasn't true. Rick had been too embarrassed to help him. Zachariah wondered how he would have reacted if it had been Rick who puked and got kicked in the nuts. He thought he would have helped Rick to the nurse.

Freshly showered, he put his clothes into the washing machine. He briefly considered going back to school. The pain in his nuts, while dulled, was still bad enough that he couldn't concentrate.

He got into bed and pulled the covers over his head. His dad usually came home around five thirty and expected dinner. He looked at the clock: twelve forty. Plenty of time.

But he was yanked from bed half an hour later.

"Why am I getting calls that you're skipping school?"

There was no alcohol on his father's breath, thank goodness, but hot rage was still inches from his face.

"Dad, I—"

"What? What was it?" Spittle hit Zachariah's cheeks.

"We were playing soccer, Dad. And I—got hit in the nuts. Really hard!"

"I don't give a damn. Everyone gets hit in the jewels. You know what you do? You MAN UP. Deal with it! You don't make me leave money at my station. You know how much your little nap costs?"

"But, Dad, when I got hit it was really bad. I—"

"Not as bad as it's gonna be."

How had he not seen the sock?

The next day, the familiar pain was there, stronger than usual. He walked deliberately, like he'd aged fifty years since the previous afternoon.

Nothing was different until he got to his locker.

Kids he didn't know walked by. Piss, some said.

Ralph, others said.

Girls tittered.

Look how slow he walks, someone said. Laughter.

Musta gotten kicked real hard.

More laughter.

On his desk in study hall, first period, the word "piss" was written on his desk in block letters.

A paper football, flipped onto his desk from somewhere behind: PISS TIETZ.

How had everyone found out?

In every class now, and in the hallway to and from them, someone calling him either Ralph or Piss. And not just guys he recognized, either. Kids from the sixth and seventh grades. Guys, girls.

At lunch, Zachariah moved through the line with a cheeseburger and tater tots and a carton of lemonade on his tray.

Some kid in front of him, a little smaller, said you like lemonade? I hear you're pretty good at making it.

Zachariah bit his lip. He was bigger. But if he punched the kid he'd get sent to the principal. And then he'd get home and be in real trouble. The physical ramifications of skipping two classes had been with him all day when he turned his head too quickly or tried to walk faster than he should have. What would his dad do to him if he got in a fight?

The kid held up his own carton of lemonade.

Jim and Rick and Kenny weren't sitting at their regular table.

He found them at the far end of the cafeteria, as if they were hiding.

"Hey, guys," he said. "You moved."

Silence.

"You moved."

"Aren't you the kid who puked all over himself yesterday?"

"Very funny."

"And you pissed yourself. Right?"

"Rick, you were there."

"I saw some guy I don't know piss himself and puke."

"That was me."

Jim's tater tots held a particular fascination; Kenny watched the clock on the wall intensely.

"You know me."

"We don't know anyone who pisses himself," Rick said.

"Come on. We—"

"No one in school wants to hang out with a pisser."

"But—"

"Good luck finding someplace to sit," Rick said.

For a few days afterward, Zachariah tried eating in the cafeteria. No one was happy to see him arrive at their table. Kids from class or soccer got up and left, or didn't speak to him, or, once, told him to fuck off.

He began eating his lunch in the bathroom. At least the year is almost over, he thought. I'll be going to a new school in September, where everyone will forget this. I'll have new friends.

Then, over the summer, he gained weight—so much that his dad called the doctor.

His father was angry to take time off work, but did not beat him: the doctor would see bruises if he did. Zachariah expected— and received—payback once the appointments passed.

"This is a lot of weight for a small period of time," the doctor said. "But it is not unprecedented. It happens sometimes, usually to girls."

After answering questions about diet, sleep, and exercise, the doctor said Zachariah's added weight was a phase he would grow out of. Try to exercise more than you do, he said. It's summer, so this shouldn't be a problem. Watch your diet. Don't overdo it at barbecues.

Zachariah rode his newly uncomfortable bike what felt like fifty miles a day, all over town, hoping he'd win the Weight Loss Fitness Challenge. He tried not to eat too much. Drank a lot of water. But somehow he gained more weight. And when the school year started, no one had forgotten his accident. His weight gain made him a target for people who hadn't heard about the soccer field.

As he sat there in the library, he realized there was research to be done.

It was strange that his new bulk came in such close proximity to his powers emerging. What if both had been caused by the same thing? Maybe they had started that day, like there was some gland down there that activated when he got kicked in the nuts. The Internet had to have something on psychic powers, right?

10.

DIDN'T WANT TO GET THERE TOO early. Sit around and talk to people he didn't know. But not too late either. Get a good seat. Nod to people around him. Not talk. Maybe after a big play. But that was it.

He left at six fifteen for seven. Half hour walk. If he remembered right. Didn't go down there much. Didn't like to think about it. Wasn't good at it. Tried to concentrate. Couldn't. And this was before. Wished he had done voc, like Artie. Good stuff. Jobs. But Auntie Blake said college prep. Which he hated. But she took him in so she was the boss. He said okay. Tried hard. For a long time. Two years. But never any good. Stopped trying so hard. Did about the same. Cs and Ds turned into Ds and Fs. She sighed loudly and said well, some people just aren't cut out for a better life. He remembered that. A better life. His would have been better if he did cars. Kids in classes gave him looks. Didn't even apply for school after that. Or scholarships. Said he'd work. Keep his mill job. But layoffs. So he joined up.

Walked down in the dark. Streetlights along the way. Not like the way to Schaferville. No sidewalks. Barely a shoulder. The school walk was easy. Leg doing okay. Saw other people headed there. Big paper signs under their arms.

Full parking lot. Band playing in the background. Felt a headache coming behind his eyes. Maybe it would be okay.

Still there, but a little less. It would be okay.

Less.

Okay.

He looked up. Away from the people. Bugs swarming lights. Getting too cold for them. That morning he woke up to ice puddles. First all year. Winter coming. Tired of global warming. Wasn't true. Especially in his apartment. Felt cold air through the walls. Birds flying south. In packs. Flocks. Leaves mostly already gone. Saw his breath. Wasn't the first time for that, but still. First ice. Long winter. Last year in the desert. Hot all the time. Except night. Couldn't believe how cold it got. But his apartment. January would suck. February. Go to the library all day. Probably still walk.

Garages cold in the winter. Artie, his hands must freeze. Probably had a space heater. Warm them up. Go in the office. Keep customers warm. Hoped he didn't have to talk to them. Just wanted to fix stuff. Get paid. But he might like telling them. Like look at the score marks on the clutch plate. I'm glad we replaced it when we did the timing belt. He could do that. As long as it wasn't that'll be eight hundred even all the time. Money made him nervous. Math was okay. Until the really hard stuff. But being that guy, that was Artie. He was good at it. Always. Easy to hang around him. Planning. Organizing.

Bleachers were full mostly except the visitors' and the back. He didn't want to sit on the Hanley side, get looks. Hey, what are you doing over there? I thought you were one of us. If anyone even recognized him.

Packed at the bottom. Kids being stupid, probably drunk. Reminded him of himself. Before he went over. Walked up, feeling eyes roll off. Way up there was space.

Middle of an empty row, second from the back. Looked around. Kids, families. One guy with no shirt. Painted white. Kid next to him. Painted blue. Shivering.

What the fuck. Come on, Dad. Kid's cold. Even through the fat. Shoulders on him slumped. Sitting there freezing. No energy. Didn't want to be there.

The band came on. Played a song. Recognized it a little. Something new. Liked it. But he missed the old stuff. Easier to guess the next one. The ba-na-na-na-na-na-na-na-HEY song. They still played that, right?

Stands kept filling. He couldn't see spaces. Where people were going. Just not up the stairs. Which was okay. If some hot chick sat next to him, great. But there weren't any. Only wives and girl-friends. If he were a hot chick, he'd sit next to him. Be like hey.

The kid shivering. Standing now, clapping. Like his dad. The people around, their heads kept turning to them, nodding. Like yeah. How could they not see it? The kid was cold! Didn't want to be there.

National anthem. Stood. A tape. No singer. Everyone had hands over hearts. Some men saluted. He saluted. Never used to care. Before he went.

He hadn't been sure. Thought it would be okay. No loud noises. Plenty of space. Okay. So far, anyway. Headache gone. Anthem helped. Didn't think it would.

Teams came on. Band playing music he knew. Intro music. They ran. Pointed at the sky. Jumped up and down. Hit each other in the helmet.

Hanley ran on. Looked like the fat kid. No spring.

He didn't get it. Football was hard. Those kids hated it. He could tell. And he was sitting far away. If he could see, so could Armbrister High. Hanley was going to get their asses kicked.

Armbrister deferred. They kicked to the five. Good one. On the first play Hanley got stripped. A back yanked the ball from the running back. Clear even from where he sat. The crowd yelled UVVVVV. Back picked it up and ran it in. But not really ran. Twenty feet. But still. Touchdown.

Hanley slumped like they wanted it even less. The crowd cheered.

So did the fat kid. Flabby painted arms in the air. But it was show.

Armbrister kicked again. Pinned them back again. Crowd doing UVVVVVV. Except what was the kid's name? From the newspaper. The good one.

Did the fat kid have friends? Maybe. There was a fat kid in his class. What was his name? Funny guy. Fat kids had to be. Defend yourself. Make everyone laugh. Flip it. Like ha, I'm fat. Except the ha was fake.

Roy couldn't flip his thing. Tried. Everyone knew. From the beginning. But him. When did it start—second grade? Third? Somewhere in there. The first few times he tried. Forget it. But it was true. That was the thing. If it was yeah you're fat he could be like ha, yeah. But they knew even though he didn't all the way. Didn't understand. Not yet. Not until then. Asked Auntie Blake. She didn't answer. Said just ignore them. So he knew.

And it got worse. First it was your mom shops at Salvation Army. She did. So did Auntie Blake. But the kids with nice clothes said that. New sneakers. Sweaters. So that made it bad. It didn't bother him until he understood it was supposed to.

Then it was your mom's on food stamps. Which she was. A small kid said it to him. He punched the small kid. Went to the office. The principal saying why did you do that, Roy? Because he said my mother was on food stamps. Just ignore them, he said. And it will go away. Couldn't say I've been trying to ever since they said my mother shops at Salvation Army and it didn't go away it got worse so I got mad and hit one so now it will go away. Because the principal would never say hit people. Even if it was fair.

So it stopped for a few days. Detention. Auntie Blake shaking her head. Roy, she said, you must rise above this foolishness. Your roots.

But then it started again. And the kid was bigger. Like normal-sized. And he punched back.

It hurt. But it wasn't bad. He could get hit. And hit back. That was his first real fight. A tie. Neither of them stopped. Kept going until they were both pulled away. An art teacher. Scarves. Smelled like stuff you put in a bathroom to cover shit. You boys! What are you doing to each other? Like it had never happened before. Like she had never seen it before. Maybe she hadn't. Maybe that's why she was so scared.

Every few days was like that. A fight, detention. Stantz's office. But if he didn't fight it would be every day. He won at first. Smaller kids. And some big kids. And he lost some. The small ones stopped talking to his face. Just behind his back. At lunch, in class. He thought it would never end. It made Artie mad.

And it got worse. First it was about crack. Before he knew what it was. He fought about that.

Then after. He never thought it would be so bad. Not because he was sad. He wasn't. Which made him feel guilty. Auntie Blake saying it was okay for him to get in touch with his feelings. To let it all out. But he was. And it pissed him off. That he became a bigger target. So he fought better. Not like just enough to end it like usual. Like I am going to hurt you. Fucking break you in half. Only a few kids. New ones. After his mother died and he sent that kid to the hospital they left him alone. Pretty much. Still something said sometimes. Behind his back. Always felt it even if there was nothing to hear. Felt looks.

After the first one he won, his first fight win, the little kid got up eventually. Walked away slumped. Like the fat kid. His shoulders said fuck with me. Hit me again. Harder. Roy used to stand like that. Figured it out as the kid walked away. So he stood in front of the mirror at home. Wanted to try it right then at school but someone would have seen him doing it in the bathroom. Laugh. Another fight. Didn't want that. So he practiced. At home.

He wished he could go back and tell the kid in the mirror about Peck.

Hanley kicked. Armbrister returned it all the way to the twenty.

The guy jumped up and down. The kid pretended. Still slumped. Maybe he wanted his dad to think he liked it.

He wanted to say hey, fat kid, look. At least he's here. That was another thing. Fights, chants. *Who's Your Daddy?* A bunch of them. First it was pick out the smallest. But the big ones would come at him all at once. So it was the biggest from then on. Everyone stopped to watch. Surprised. Got his ass kicked sometimes. Stantz and detention. But not all the time. It slowed down.

He talked to her while she was in the hospital. Went in. Needed to know. Couldn't remember much from growing up with her. Mostly a lot of TV. People in and out. Which made sense. He didn't know then. He just watched TV. Reruns. *Brady Bunch*. Brothers and sisters. Mom and Dad.

He could hear the bus down the road over the TV set. Sometimes he went. His mom would wake up and say go to school. But she didn't mean it. Not like when she said do those dishes. Or stay in your room. Or clean this shit. She was saying it because she had to. Wouldn't hit him. Too tired. So he waited for her to go back to sleep and watched more TV. The bus at the trailer park entrance waiting less and less.

Then Auntie Blake. Her sisters. Dusty old house. Smelly. Different smells. Didn't know the trailer smell names until later.

Auntie Blake always meant it when she said go. He said okay and went back to sleep. Or tried to. Royal, she'd say, it's time for you to get up. And she'd yank the covers off. I am not saying this to hear myself talk.

Thanksgiving one year. The first one, must've been. The only one. Some huge dude. Smoked in the house. Please extinguish your cigarette, Auntie Blake said. Tattoos. Mustache. Smelled like a garage and something else. Get me an ashtray. I will not be spoken to in that way in my own house, she said. Picked up the turkey platter and went to the kitchen. His mom went in after her. The guy smoked to the filter. Ground it out on his plate.

Kitchen yelling. Some old lady took him outside. One of the aunts. Tried to get him to play. Didn't want to. Could hear them yelling inside. Couldn't hear words.

His mom and the guy came out. Not running. But mad. Looked like she was dragging him. Big strong guy pulled by a lady. Went right past. Didn't say anything. Wanted her to. Goodbye. Happy Thanksgiving. See you soon. But she didn't. They got into a huge loud car. Drove away.

Hanley returned it to the ten. Then a sack. UVVVVVVV except it was DOVVVVVVE. That was it. From the newspaper. Ross Dove.

Guy jumping up and down. Fat kid trying to give a shit. Did they paint for every game? He wouldn't try so hard if this was his first one. He'd be like look at me, I'm doing this. I'm painted. He slumped like he wanted to disappear.

Went to see her. His great aunt said I understand why you're going, Royal, but no good will come of it.

I just need to—

I understand. But prepare yourself. Nothing good will come of it. Believe me.

Why would she say that? He had to go.

He understood later.

Tubes in her nose. Taped to her arm. Beeps. Noises. Skeleton in a bed. She tried to breathe every time. Couldn't just breathe. Eyes closed.

Sat there. Held her hand. Waited for her to wake up. Open her eyes. Something. But she didn't. Trying to pull breaths. No one else in the room. A TV playing down the hall. Wanted to say something. Yell. Don't you know what's happening? But they did. So TVs.

He sat and waited and she never opened her eyes.

Went back a few times. Didn't tell Auntie Blake.

She was awake once. Looked at him. Didn't see him, though. Couldn't tell. He said it's me and she made a noise. That was it. He tried to think if she told him something and he couldn't remember and should have been paying attention to what she said instead of watching TV. But he watched because he didn't want to know. Even then. The *Brady Bunch* and all the families on TV who went places and did things and sat together and ate the same food at the same time weren't the reason even though he liked to think of all that stuff. Wasn't how it was with Auntie Blake. Always sighing. Not because she was tired. She didn't like him. Felt like she had to take care of him. Charity case. And he couldn't do honors. Didn't care enough. Wanted to. Maybe she'd like him more. But he couldn't. School, work at night, sleep. So.

Kickoff again. The back ran it to midfield. The guy was happy. The kid was not. Hanley had no chance. He could go home. Or play pool. But no one went to Patterson's during games. So he had to stay. Or his apartment by himself.

A pass. Forty-something yards. The guy jumped. High-fived his kid. Who didn't care. But tried to. For his dad.

11.

THE GAME IS TONIGHT. I'M GONNA meet up with those guys. I hope Mary is there.

* * *

Oh my God I feel sick. My head feels like it's gonna explode.

* * *

I'm gonna barf.

* * *

(gap in tape)

* * *

I left the recorder out last night. Next to the bed. Anyone could have come in and found it.

I guess this is a hangover.

It sucks.

Don was out in the living room when I got up. I musta barfed like three or four times. I thought he was gonna hit me. When I went to the kitchen I had to walk by him. He started laughing and said you have the virus, huh?

I was like I don't know what you're talking about.

He laughed again and said a girl like you never had the virus before?

I didn't get it.

He said you have a hangover. You drank too much at the game.

When I said I wasn't hungover he laughed even louder. Oh please, he said. I could smell it all the way down the hall. Whiskey and beer.

He was right. Wine, too.

He said I could tell even before you started yakking. You were something at the game.

Did I see him there?

He said you don't remember. Boy, you tied one on.

Then he said don't think you're off the hook. Your mother will be home soon. Then we'll talk.

When I asked about what, he said school. And the crowd you're running with.

I started to tell him I'm not running with a crowd but he cut me off and said you probably don't remember half of what you did last night. There are more important things than yourself, you got that?

I said like what, my brother?

He stood up and said family. Then, you need to show more respect.

I said you're not part of this family, without even thinking. It just came out of my mouth. And before I knew it I was on the floor.

Something was on my chin. I felt it.

Blood from my lip.

I wish I had taped it. I could play it for Mom. Or the cops.

He said you don't remember how you got that.

You just hit me, asshole.

He said no, you don't remember. Because you blacked out. Drank too much. One of those boys did this. Or you fell down.

I said no, this was you. You did this. And I almost got up.

He said you didn't hear me, did you?

I stayed down.

He said this family's got enough to worry about without you making an ass of yourself. Or failing out. Then he said get up.

I said I never fail out.

He said your mother hasn't seen a report card. Why not?

I didn't say anything.

You hid it. Or burned it.

He was right.

Then he said get up.

I went why, so you can hit me again?

He said maybe. Keep hanging with that crowd and you'll wind up in jail. They'll do way worse to you there.

I said no.

He kicked me and was like your mother spoils the shit out of you. That's why you're like this. You need some discipline. I know about discipline, believe me.

I couldn't breathe.

I tried to say something, but I couldn't.

He said you don't remember that, either. 'Course, your mother won't see that one. One of your boyfriends might. Slut. You tell them you don't remember what happened. You blacked out.

It took a while before I could breathe again. When I could I stood up.

He said cut the shit, you hear me?

* * *

I don't remember all of it. But there are parts I do.

I met those guys at the Pines. Steve and Earl. Arnold and Gil and Kelly, who I guess goes out with Gil. They made out all night. And Mary.

Their cars were parked outside a house. I went in and like always Steve said what's up, Dixon? and threw me a beer.

I drank it fast. I guess I was nervous. I felt it hit me.

He said you excited for the game? I was like yeah, whatever.

Steve told everyone that Ross was my brother and they looked at me different. Mary said I heard he's going to some big school and I was like yeah, maybe.

I saw she had this look on her face like she already knew the answers but was gonna ask the questions anyway. Because it was me. I was cool with that.

She said there's always college people at practices. I said you guys go? She laughed and said yeah. Nothing else to do.

The guys all wanted me to drink flasks. I did. I thought it would make talking to Mary easier. I don't like whiskey. It warmed me up, though.

They started passing a joint. It came to me and I hit it and passed it to Mary.

Everyone was talking about school and how hard it was to find jobs. The guys said the only way to get out of town was to join up but then you might come home in a bag. I started talking about restaurant row. Gil said I should talk to some guy named Gary at the Burger Hut. Kelly was like God, that guy is gross. The guys laughed and Earl said if I really wanted work I could talk to him. I told Earl I put in a resume and everyone laughed. He said Dixon's too good for an application! Mary said I think it's smart.

The joint came around. I hit it again and when I passed it Mary started asking about English class. She moved here from Maine. She told me about concerts she went to.

So we stood there for a while talking and it felt good. It started to get dark and Steve was like ready to go? We got in two cars.

Steve was driving one and that guy Arnold was in the other. I started to get in with Arnold but Mary grabbed my hand and pulled me over to Steve's car. Earl was in the front seat. Steve lit another joint and passed it to Earl, who passed it to Mary, who passed it to me. I hit it and almost dropped it when I passed it up because Mary took my hand.

The whole ride the guys were talking up front. I was, too, to Mary. It was like watching a recording of a conversation I was in. I could feel my mouth moving but I didn't know what I was going to say next. I guess I was surprised. I thought a lot of what I said was cool. But I can't remember what I was talking about.

We got there and parked. I remember being kinda scared that Mom would be there with Don. They do Saturday afternoon games sometimes, but she works Fridays. And Don doesn't usually go by himself. But as we went to the bleachers I kept thinking about it. It was like I was stuck. What if they got off early? Would they see me? It was hard not to think like that.

I didn't know what was happening with the game. All I knew was that I had to watch out for my brother when the defense was on the field. Number fifty-four. I remember him being happy about his number because some guy named Beer Can on the Patriots used to have it. I elbowed Mary and said that. She thought it was funny. When I did the same to Earl he passed me a flask.

Ross stuck up his hand and knocked the ball down. I started clapping and yelling. People got into it. Everyone was doing ROSS! DOVE! ROSS! DOVE! After a while they were cheering for me, not for him. Steve kept yelling SHE'S ROSS DOVE'S SISTER! and people would all clap. Mary thought it was wicked funny. She said you're usually so quiet. I felt myself smile.

It was fun hanging out but I don't know what happened. I mean, I think they won, but I don't know why or how. Someone gave me a water bottle full of warm beer and I split it with Mary, and the wine they poured into plastic juice bottles, and the flask. I drank everything.

Things got fuzzy.

I remember some stuff but not in order.

I was in front of the whole bleachers, pointing at one side yelling ROSS and the other yelling DOVE and everyone was yelling with me. That was awesome.

Then we were back in cars, going to the Pines.

Mary was laughing. That was after the game.

Someone had a flashlight. We walked from the Pines to the quarry. There was more beer. And a box of wine. And a joint. Mary laughed at things I said but can't remember.

Then I was home.

I want to go to all of the games.

But I need to figure out how not to puke. I'll look at the library.

My brain feels slow. Like my thoughts need to get through a big sponge before they come out.

I hope I see Mary in school Monday.

12.

ZACHARIAH SHIVERED, WISHING HIS DAD THOUGHT shirts were
weather-appropriate. He felt the chill of fall despite his new weight.
He had worried throughout the summer about the implications of
his newfound bulk: would his dad be excessively optimistic about
his son's warmth because of his newfound poundage? The answer,
unfortunately, was yes. Time and again, Zachariah removed body
paint from fresh flab with cold cream he had bought with his
meager allowance. The addition of so much surface area to his
frame meant new and exotic places for leftover blue and white to
hide. Any paint he didn't remove yielded an itchy rash the next day,
inevitably left unattended because of awkward location: under-
arms, stomach rolls, and, worst, under his newly acquired sagging
breasts. No matter how thorough his post-game removal sessions,
he always managed to miss some.

The playoffs were growing closer, and the team, with its lone
loss to Schaferville, seemed a lock. The bleachers began to fill with
faces out of context—familiar from the halls, yet alien to games.

Like Dixon.

Zachariah couldn't believe his stupidity. She shouted at the
crowd from the front of the bleachers in the second quarter. What

did she care about the defense? Of all people, why would Dixon—with her smell and snarl—attend a football game? Had she sought him out for further humiliation?

No.

As she screamed, Paul Tietz rolled his eyes. "Gotta watch out for girls like that," he said. "Nothing but trouble. Can your believe her?"

"No," Zachariah said, thinking *she's been giving me titty twisters pretty much every week since school started. She tore up one of my notebooks—not the game show one, thank God—and threw it up in the air right by her locker, near the front door. Everyone saw. Except for the ancient security guard who was always standing there. How did he not see it? And she pushed me into the girls' bathroom. But nothing since my powers started a few weeks ago.*

He had a momentary, reckless urge to tell his father about the end of the Schaferville game, how his newfound abilities had manifested and had kept him safe since (though its boundaries did not extend to verbal attacks—or to his father).

"He's gonna go All-State," his father said, nodding his head toward one of the players on the sideline. "Maybe All-New England. Even when we won the whole thing, we didn't have anyone go All-New England."

Zachariah nodded.

"I hope you appreciate what you're seeing here," Paul said. "This kid has a chance to go pro. When he does, you can tell your kids that Ross Dove played right here at Armbrister High. First player in town to get to the big show."

The defense ran onto the field after a punt. As if on cue, Dixon appeared in front of the bleachers.

"That girl again," Paul Tietz said.

She pointed at one side of the bleachers. They yelled with her. Then the other side yelled something else.

"At least she has good taste," Paul said.

"What do you mean?"

"She's having everyone yell Ross Dove's name," he said.

Zachariah felt sick.

He listened to the crowd: ROSS! DOVE! ROSS! DOVE!

Dixon.

Dove.

Oh no.

He'd heard both names used together around the halls, but somehow never made the connection. Dixon Dove.

Ross Dove was her brother.

She'd be at all the games.

It was bad enough being called Piss all the time. And he hated wearing makeup. If Dixon—Dixon Dove—saw him at a game, Zachariah felt sure she would make his time at school even worse.

I hope she never sees me at a game, he thought.

Then: *I just used my power.*

He'd be careful. He had to be. In the back of his mind was the nagging suspicion that he had no powers; maybe the pass hadn't been picked off because of his mind. Maybe it was just the right guy in the right place at the right time.

But he believed in it. More than anything, he wanted to believe it. And wanting it so badly was part of the process. Right? It had to be, in the same way that working on *Love Balloon* would get him out of Armbrister. Had to.

Believing didn't mean he could live dangerously, though. At school he'd continued to spend time in the library rather than the cafeteria, where he knew—powers or no—that kids would make his life miserable.

The powers were like an insurance policy, maybe. A safety net.

He couldn't get out of going to games with his dad. He knew that. But hopefully his powers would protect him from being embarrassed by Dixon Dove at a game. Zachariah imagined his father's anger: *You're gonna let a girl treat you like that? Don't you have a pair?*

Down front, Dixon Dove continued motioning to the bleachers, leading the crowd in chanting her brother's name.

Her brother. He felt the knowledge in his stomach.

"Do you know her?"

"I've seen her around school," Zachariah said.

"Girls like her are nothing but trouble," his dad said. "Stay away from her."

Zachariah was happy to say he would.

13.

ONLY WAY TO GET IN SHAPE to walk was walking. Apartment too small for exercise. Woke up and did push-ups and sit-ups. Crunches. Not enough. Cheap place. Floor might cave in if he did jumping jacks.

Thought about a gym. Could barely pay bills. Far away. Would need to drive. Didn't want to. Felt a headache behind his eyes thinking about it. Wouldn't walk home sweaty. Freeze like that. So he just walked. Laps around the common. To the woods. By the quarry. Saw another deer up there.

Had some deer once. Guy his mom dated. Only one he liked. John. Garbage man. Smelled a little. Can't ever wash it off, he said. Not all the way. But for twenty-two an hour you take it.

He brought some venison over. And a little grill. Cooked it up. Mom made potatoes. Frozen beans. Tasted so good. Still remembered. Eight, maybe. Wanted to say keep this one. Not yell all the time. Eat good food. Throw a baseball. Holidays. All the stuff on TV. But real. But he stopped coming. Not right away. But close. A week, maybe? Two?

One morning he got tired of common laps. Seeing the same things. Leg still hurt but fuck it. He'd go. To Schaferville. Ask Artie if they needed help. Finally.

Up one hill, down another. The entire way. Felt his breath. Sucking air.

Basic. All the running. Fifteen miles. Packs. Up hills. Back down. Never got easier. Thought he was going to die. Stared straight ahead. Didn't want to scrub more bowls. What the fuck, Donaldson said. Like we're gonna have to run fifteen miles in the desert in full gear. That'll never happen. But if it does, Long said, we're ready. I will kiss McSorley square on the lips and give him a reach around if I ever have to run fifteen in the desert, Peck said. Felt a laugh come up. Bit it down. Didn't want McSorley to rip his head off.

All that gone now. Came home. Walked. Not the same. PT. Still hurt. The guys he met at the hospital said wow, you're lucky. Hard to think about.

The job would help. The garage. Be around people all day. Artie. Fix cars. Get strength.

Longer than he thought. And he thought it was long. Hours. Working late would suck. No shoulder. Cars close. Sometimes old people walked out there. They waved. He waved back. They wore reflectors. Vests, straps. Thought they looked dumb. But made sense. Night, hard to see. Didn't have light clothes. Fatigues. Sweatshirts. Navy blue. Always his favorite.

Downhill was bad. Almost worse than up. Felt it in his knees. His leg. Got rubbery. Probably the same on the way home. But worse. Have to walk it until he got a bike. But snow. Maybe Artie could drive. Wasn't far. By car. But the time. There and back. Couldn't ask. Too much.

Artie used to drive him everywhere. That car, Oldsmobile. Dead grandfather's. Boat. Shit mileage. Big backseat, though, Artie said. Elbowed him. Roy smiled, nodded. He knew. From videos. Not until basic. Weekend pass. Guys knew a place.

No money for driver's ed, Auntie Blake said. Sorry, Royal. We both know after driver's ed comes a car. And insurance. I have a job, he said. If that's the case, you'll have to learn on your own. He told Artie about it.

What a bitch, he said.

Maybe she resents it.

What, having to put you up?

She does, he said. She does. And Artie taught him to drive. I don't mind, he said. Means I can drink. You're the designated hitter. Laughed. But he didn't mind. It felt good, being useful.

Cars whizzing by. Close. Broad daylight. Didn't see him. Weren't looking. Bad road. Only way to Schaferville. Bus once a day. Noon. Why not more he didn't know. Made no sense. Back four hours later. Four. That one might work. Walk in the morning, early shift, bus home. Not bad. Sit in the same seat. Talk to the driver. Get to know him. Joke around. Meet the other people on the bus. Everyone would know he worked at the garage. Come by with their cars. Say hello, Roy. Artie's boss, whoever he was, would see him bring business. Job security.

Schaferville. Passed the sign. Incorporated 1726. Oldest town around. Up there on the river. That and Wilburton. Armbrister used to be part of Wilburton. Remembered that from school. Thaddeus Armbrister. Good American. Said no. All our kids being sent to war. None of yours. We're the poor part of town. Your kids can afford not to go. Not right. Split off. Hadn't thought much about it. Story from school. But it was true. In their platoon there was one guy who went to college. Fuckin' hated it, he said. Filling your head with bullshit. His name was—what? Hard to remember. One semester of community college and his name was College Boy. They thought that was funny. Biggest guy in the platoon. Could've played football. Didn't. Bad knees, he said. Carried the radio. Sweated like a pig. McSorley always gave him shit. So did they. Pretty funny. Hey, College Boy, Peck would say. What did your college books say about carrying a radio? Fuck you, College Boy would always say, sweating. Maybe you should have stayed in college. That way, you wouldn't have to carry a fuckin' radio all over the desert! Ever think of that? Every goddamn day. And they'd laugh at him, but not like mean. Like ha. They were all in the same boat. All in the shit. Sucked for everyone.

College Boy collapsed. Heatstroke. Got redeployed. Someone went to see him. Donaldson? Said he asked College Boy what he'd do when he got home. Oh, you know, he said. The usual. Maybe read books about bullshit. Work a job where I use my hands.

Walked through downtown Schaferville. Bookstore, coffee shop. Trophy place. Sandwiches. Some new stuff. Flowers. Beer store. Not like drinking it but making it. He wondered how to do that. How hard it would be. Make beer. Probably expensive. Big jar. Buckets. Reminded him of chemistry class. Never got that. Why he had to do that stuff. Never used it. Didn't care. Maybe chemistry made it easier to make beer. He'd ask Artie.

He kept walking. Stores with nothing inside. Tried to remember what had been in them. Couldn't. Just remembered them full. Not when he left. Before that.

Left downtown. Bigger common than Armbrister. Probably good to walk around. Tried to imagine living there. Quiet. Walk common laps. Probably expensive. Maybe not when he got hired. Find a small place. Thought he remembered a bar. Go after work. Play some pool. Drink some beer. Watch the Sox. Wouldn't have to walk so far. Or worry about the bus. Moving, though. He didn't have much. But enough. Dresser. Futon. Couldn't fit that in a car. Not even on top. Maybe rent a truck. Have enough money. U-Haul. Or Artie would help. Friends from the garage. They could do an afternoon. Easy. Pizzas afterward. Beer. Perfect. Sit in the new place. Hopefully the porch. Sit out there. Sweaty, like College Boy. The first beer would be the best.

Saw a bar. Looked nice. Too nice. Like drinks instead of beers. And not Venerable. The kind from that beer store. People would drink it and talk about how it tasted. Never understood that. Beer is beer. And those places never had pool tables. He'd have to find someplace else to play. Maybe the whole town didn't have a table. He'd have to go back to Patterson's.

Fun to think about. Probably too expensive. Cheaper to have a car. Drive every day. Wouldn't be bad. One tank a month. Listen to news. No music. Back and forth. Keep playing pool. For fun. Maybe beer money. Cashing checks at the bank. Hadn't seen his check yet. Probably some holiday. That happened. Columbus Day, Presidents' Day. Pushed back the pay. Veterans Day. He would do that one. Find a parade. Get dressed up. Talk about it. Go to some bar. Get beers. Venerable.

City part ended. Trees. Rows of houses. Never looked at them before. Maybe nicer than his. But not by much. But these had siding. Not shingles. Warm in the winter. Wouldn't be hot during the summer. Find a vet landlord. Tell him just getting back on my feet. You understand. And he would. No need for a deposit, soldier. Your word is good with me. Worry less.

Then it was more stores. Empty. Not like downtown. Standalones. Garages, gas stations. Plywood over windows. Graffiti. WESTSIDE KINGS. DEAD TREND. MIZST LIVES. Didn't understand. People always needed gas. How could they not? Always had cars. Had to be bad.

Trash on the sidewalk. Then it ended. Then nothing. He turned around. Downtown still visible. After work. Walking through this part. He could handle it. Knew fighting. Killed sand niggers. Wasn't scared much. But it looked rough. Maybe he'd pack. A knife. Brass knuckles. Didn't have a pistol. Just the old rifle.

Mrs. Johnson. He went back to the house. Thought one of the great-aunts would be there. Sold. Didn't even go in. Could tell. The cars. Hybrids. She came out of her house. On the porch. Why, Royal, she said. Is that you? Yes, Missus Johnson, he said. Oh, you must be back from overseas! I just got back, he said. Didn't mention the hospital. That counted as back. I am very sorry about Blake, she said. She was a kind soul. Yes ma'am, he said. I have something for you inside, she said. Wait here. She came back out with the rifle in its camo bag. Glenda and Joan did not know what to do with this, she said. They did not want to sell it, but did not want to keep it. I told them I'd hold it for you. Thank you, ma'am, he said. I hope you are well, Royal, she said. Do let me know if there is anything I can do for you. He felt like saying well I'm having a hard time. I have no place to stay and my one friend is married. So if I could stay here while I get it together that'd be great. But he couldn't do that. She would say yes. He knew. Always nice to him. Offered him cookies until he was sixteen. Probably because he always took them. Husband died young. Construction accident. Never remarried. Did a lot of church stuff. Her, Auntie Blake, Tillie Tompkins. She was nice. But she wouldn't be. She'd feel mad. Taking up space. Eating food. Coming in late. Never say anything. But hate it. Like Auntie Blake hated it. Him. No stake but a rifle. Thank you, Missus Johnson, he said, taking the bag from her. I'll do that. And never went back.

Sidewalk trash everywhere until the garage. He didn't remember this. Thought it was better. Beaters outside. Big. American. Wondered if that was all they did. One of those places. American repairs. Thought he could do that. Jeeps. Sounded good. Easy to get parts. Fords.

Electric buzzer when he walked in. Little bell tinkled in the doorway. He'd get used to both. Wouldn't hear them after a while. But would with his body. Like shots. His body knew. Found himself in the sand without thinking. Tinkle meant be nice. Someone coming in. Train himself like that. Wouldn't even have to try. Just happen over time. Hello, can I help you? Yes, your car is ready. I replaced the timing belt.

Woman came to the desk. Smelled like butts. Older. Tough broad. Help you? she said.

I'm looking for Artie, he said. Maybe she owned the place. Probably. Why else would a woman be in a garage? He stood straighter. Tired because of the walk. His leg. Should've thought of that before he came in. Didn't. Stupid.

He doesn't work Mondays, hon. Tuesday through Saturday. Need help with something?

He liked being called hon. Reminded him of diners. Wished Patterson lady called him hon when he played pool. Just told him how many beers he could drink.

No, I'm one of Artie's buddies.

What's your name?

Roy, he said.

Roy—?

Eggleton.

Well, Roy Eggleton, I'll tell him you were asking after him. Try back tomorrow or some other time this week.

He nodded.

Not working. All that way. For nothing. Pretty fucking stupid not to call first.

14.

I DITCHED AFTER NINTH PERIOD TO get a bike and see Gary.

He's older than Don. That didn't stop him from staring at my tits.

He seemed surprised when I told him I already applied. He went what did you say your name was again? Then I told him and he said oh, okay, I didn't realize.

He took out a huge stack of applications and looked through. When he found mine he said nice resume and I said thanks. Then he said when can you start, Dixon Dove? I said whenever you want. He asked what my availability was and I said after school and weekends. He said he'd give me a call if there were any openings.

* * *

Mr. Merrill gave me a bunch of shit for not doing the reading. Whatever. It's like, who the fuck cares what a bunch of made-up people in a story do, anyway? It's not like Burger Hut will call back because of that stuff.

But Don was sitting on his fat ass today when I got home and he said you better from that virus? I hadn't seen him since Saturday. He said what did you learn and I said what? He goes what did you learn from being hungover?

Without thinking I said I need to hide it better.

He stood up and said that is exactly what I'm talking about. I was like calm down, Don, and he said I will not calm down. Not with you making an ass of yourself at a game in front of recruiters.

I guess I should've known.

So I said okay, I'll remember to take it easy and he hit me. I fell down.

He goes you remember that. And this, too: your brother thinks he wants to go to Nebraska, and the recruiters flew out here to watch him again, you understand that? Scouts don't fly for nothing. Especially to a shitty town like Armbrister, you hear me? I started to say yeah, Armbrister's pretty shitty, but I thought he'd hit me again. Or kick me, maybe.

I said I hear you.

He goes so we're at the game after we both got time off to watch your brother play the game of his life when his teenage sister staggers out of the crowd shitfaced. You understand that?

I said yeah.

He goes yeah, what?

Yeah, I understand.

He said I bet you don't remember a lot from that night.

He's right, too. I hate that. But he is.

He said you're hanging out with a bunch of boys, getting loaded. You're gonna wind up knocked up. And you know who will have to support your slutty ass? Me, that's who.

Without thinking about it I said you don't support shit. I saw him get mad but I had enough time to move before he tried to kick me. I rolled across the floor. That made him even madder. I was like my mom supports you, and you think my brother's gonna support you when he goes pro.

He kinda took a running kick at me. I could feel all the air leave when his foot hit. How is a guy who spends all his time on the couch so fast?

He said listen, you little shit. You're not gonna talk to me like that.

I couldn't breathe.

If you had discipline in your life you wouldn't talk to me like that. You'd respect your elders.

I still couldn't breathe. I could feel his foot in my stomach and his handprint across my face.

I tried to talk and nothing came out a bunch of times. When something did I said I'm gonna tell my mother.

He didn't look scared. He said grow the fuck up, Dixon. Take some responsibility. You fucked up.

You kicked me.

You fucked up, he said. If your brother doesn't get into Nebraska because of you it'll get even worse. You understand?

What was he gonna do, kick me out? He'd be doing me a favor.

And just because your mother won't discipline you doesn't mean I won't. And she knows that already.

* * *

The bike was behind the house the whole time Don was kicking my ass. I kept thinking about how he'd hit me more for having it. But he didn't know.

I grabbed the M-80s and Silver Salutes and put them in my bag on my way out the door.

First I biked over to the Pines. I was hoping Mary would be there. She wasn't. No one was. I think maybe no one is except for nights and weekends. Every time I go there are more butts and broken bottles. I looked around for a roach but couldn't find one.

I went into one of the houses and lit a Silver Salute but I didn't really care. I knew what was gonna happen. Same as always. An M-80, too. I taped them, but I erased it.

So instead I biked to the supermarket. There were more empty parking spaces there than I thought.

I checked door handles and they were all open. I got all kinds of stuff: a GPS, an iPhone, and an iPad! I never had one of those before. It's cool-looking. And the best part is I found a purse. Like a whole purse, just sitting there. If you're going shopping, why would you leave your purse in the car? It makes no sense. But they did. Or, she did. Jocelyn O'Donohugh. That's the name on the card. I also got sixty bucks.

From there I went to the L'il Bee to see if Ding was there. He wasn't.

I didn't want to take the bike home again because of Don, so I took it to school and thought I'd walk home.

But on the way back I saw Mary leaving.

She said hey, what are you doing? I said just going for a walk. She said do you wanna get high? and I said yeah, so we went down to the L'il Bee and back up the quarry path.

She said let's stop at the hearse.

We passed her joint back and forth on the way up there. She was talking about school. I said do you wanna see something cool? She said okay. I got out an M-80 and her eyes got all big. She asked me where I got it, and I told her I know a guy. She laughed and said who? All mysterious-like I was like I can't tell you. I laughed. She did, too.

When we got to the hearse I asked where we should light it off. She said maybe in here and held up a Poweraid bottle. It had a wide mouth. I was like that's perfect. I lit the M-80 and dropped it into the bottle. We hid behind the hearse, watching when it blew up and shredded the bottle. All that was left was the top and bottom. She laughed and grabbed my hand when it went off and asked if I had any more. I did. She let go of my hand and we looked for another bottle. There weren't any more in the hearse or on the ground, just broken glass.

She said what about the hearse?

We decided on under the hood. We both had to lift it because it was heavy and kinda rusted shut.

I lit another one and put it on the engine, which was hard because I could only use one hand because the hood was so heavy, and we dropped it shut.

I thought it might go out, but it went off with a noise that sounded even louder than usual. The hood kinda poofed out a little.

We both laughed and laughed. She said that was awesome and hugged me.

I could hear myself talking without knowing what I was gonna say next. I was telling her that my guy has all kinds of cool shit and I went down to the Pines to blow things up. Boards and stuff. You could see scorch marks on wood. She said every time we come to the hearse from now on we'll remember today when we see the hood. Even though I don't want to remember fucking Don kicking me.

I started telling Mary but I got off track and told her I was tired of living at my mom's and I wanted to drop out and get a job but my mom's boyfriend would kick my ass if I did. She said I wanna drop out, too. School's stupid. She said I could sleep on her brother's couch. He delivers pizzas. Sometimes he buys her beers. I said that's cool. Who else has a place? She said Steve and Earl. It's awesome. Gross, though. Like they never clean and there's always beer cans everywhere. Arnold has one, too. Same thing. Why can't boys ever clean up?

She started laughing. So did I.

She kinda put her hand on my side where Don kicked me. I jumped back and she said oh, I'm sorry I thought and I was like no, it's not that and pulled my shirt up. The bruise looked pretty gross and she made a noise and said that's horrible, who did that to you? I told her my mom's boyfriend. She touched it really soft and said that's terrible and kinda leaned in and then we were kissing.

I wanted to be like I'm not a dyke. But I liked it. I like her. I want her to like me.

So we kissed for a while, with tongue and everything, and I felt around under her shirt even though I was like whoa, maybe I am a dyke.

She said are you okay? and I was like yeah. Then without thinking I was like I have some shit to show you and went in my bag. She said more fireworks? I pulled out the iPad. She said oh, cool, I didn't know you had one of those. I was like I didn't, until an hour ago. She said what? and I told her about getting what I can to help move out. About the supermarket parking lot. She said I never did that and I was like it's easy. She asked me if I ever worry about fingerprints. I told her no. I never thought of that. I should wipe door handles. Or get some gloves.

She said she should get going. She went over to the hood and rubbed her hand across the bump where the M-80 was.

When we went back to the L'il Bee Ding was there. I was like my guy is here and she said that guy? and started laughing. I was like what? and she said never mind, see you at school. And she left. I wanted to ask her when I would see her again but I didn't.

I got in Ding's car.

He said was that you a while ago?

I said I don't know what you're talking about but I started laughing. I couldn't help it. He asked who else was back there and I said Mary Hawkins. He said how was her shit? I said good. He asked if I wanted some shit better than hers. I said no, I wanted money. He kinda sat up and said what do you have in mind? and I went into my bag and got the phone.

Oh, he said.

I was like yeah, I got this and some other stuff. Check it out. Then I took out the iPad. I saved the credit card for last.

He said the thing about cards is they get reported stolen fast. Like right when a person notices. You can fill your tank or get some beer but it's not like you can use it for more than that.

He said I should throw it down a drain.

I asked how much for everything and he said let's see. You sure you don't want some real good shit? Or fireworks?

I said I told you, cash.

You in trouble?

I said I was saving to move.

He said let me know if you ever wanna make some real money.

15.

HE STANDS WEARING A MICROPHONE, THIN in a pinstripe suit and smiling, the youngest in history. His success—both writing and hosting his own smash game show—is marveled over by the American public. Who knew such a talent could originate in, of all places, a depressed New Hampshire mill town?

"Welcome back to *Love Balloon!* I'm your host, Zack Fox."

A panning shot of the live studio audience, cheering wildly.

"Our ten remaining contestants have a difficult challenge today."

Five of the men stand on the floor, the other five on risers. Zack Fox stands between them and a screen bearing the face of an attractive blonde woman.

She speaks: "I don't think I'm hard to please, but I know what I like. And it's a blend of indoor and outdoor activities."

Cut to the contestants, nodding.

"So, your challenge today will test your skills and memory. The winner will be awarded five hundred points."

The contestants look at each other, smiling. Five hundred points! This challenge is the most valuable one so far.

Cut to a close-up of a guy who looks like a soccer striker. He sits in front of the TV show's heart-shaped balloon logo. He says,

"Five hundred points! I'll be able to outbid anyone. Best square, here I come!"

Cut to a close-up of a normal, heavy-set guy in front of the same logo. He's wearing a plain T-shirt. Strikers don't have acne like he does, or big thick glasses. He says to the camera, "If I win five hundred points I can wait until the first batch of contestants burns through their points buying single squares and then get the leftovers inexpensively."

"Contestants," Zack Fox says back at the studio, between the screen and the contestants, "are you ready for your next *Love Balloon* challenge?" The crowd cheers as the men nod and yell, "YEAH!"

The show's theme music plays as the contestants form a line.

"Your challenge," Zack Fox says, "is to answer Jenna's questions correctly, using these weighted balls to do so." Here Zack Fox holds one up; it is bright, and slightly larger than a softball. "For each question you answer correctly—by throwing a ball into the correct bucket—you will earn five points. The contestant with the most points will win five hundred. In the event of a tie, the contestants may elect to split the pot, or have a tie-breaker. The three contestants with the lowest points total will face elimination."

"Are we ready?"

Again, everyone yells, "YEAH!"

"*Love Balloon* contestants—begin!"

The first man stands in line facing a row of baskets. Each has its own label: fish, chicken, beef, tofu, salad.

Zach Fox stands straddling a stripe on the floor. "The first toss is Jenna's favorite food. Jenna's favorite food, first toss."

Viewers remember that the interview with Jenna, the blonde woman, is a replay from a previous episode. She says, "I try to be very aware of my weight. I was heavy in high school, then managed to get my eating habits under control. Men never used to give me the time of day, but now they pay attention. I managed to get thin because I exercised and ate a lot of fish."

The first contestant, who looks like a striker/underwear model, stands at the line holding a ball. The crowd roars choices at him.

"Jenna looks good," he says. "She's really fit. I don't think she got that way by eating beef."

The crowd cheers.

"I'm gonna say it's lean protein that got her to where she is . . . chicken!"

He throws a ball.

Wait a minute, Zachariah Tietz thinks.

The ball hangs suspended in midair.

It's a good challenge. The strikers won't remember the details the same way as regular guys, who pay more attention. He doesn't know what the strikers think about. Like Rick, once his friend, who hadn't acknowledged him since the soccer field accident. If everyone looked past him the same way Rick did, Zachariah thinks, he wouldn't have to eat lunch in the handicapped bathroom.

Even if the ball missed its intended target of chicken, it might still go in the fish bucket, and give the striker five points.

What else could he do? For a game show to succeed, action had to be included. Physical challenges would keep people watching. But they had to be fair.

A million dollars was a huge prize. And Jenna was a pretty woman. He imagined himself winning the prize and getting to the second season. It was hard for him to conceive of such a thing, in the same way, he imagined, the other normal guys on the show would have a hard time believing their good fortune if they won. He thought the underwear models and strikers wouldn't appreciate what they had, the same way Rick didn't.

And Zachariah knew he couldn't assume the strikers would forget everything Jenna said. Some of them were probably pretty smart. Rick could remember numbers in a way he couldn't—batting averages, home runs, that sort of thing. Of course, Zachariah wasn't much of a baseball fan. But he did love baking, and couldn't remember how many quarts were in a gallon, or teaspoons in a tablespoon. If Rick could do it, some of the strikers could, too. And some of the normal guys couldn't.

But it had to be fair. Zachariah couldn't tip the scales away from the strikers. In the library, he read about a fifties quiz show where answers were given to contestants ahead of time. The public outcry against the show—and against game shows in general—had been huge. Zachariah's *Love Balloon* would change the genre forever, and hopefully give a normal guy a chance with a great woman like Jenna. But the risk remained that a striker would win it all.

It had to be fair, but that didn't mean it couldn't be broken, the way *Press Your Luck* had been. Maybe there was a pattern. And maybe the normal guys would find a way to succeed.

The physical challenges would balance the mental ones, which he thought the normal guys would win.

It would work. He had to trust that the normal guys would succeed if given the same chance as the strikers.

The ball, hanging in midair, comes alive and lands in the "chicken" basket.

The next contestant, a normal guy, walks to the stripe.

"I think Bob's right," he says, gesturing toward the previous contestant. "I think she likes chicken the best."

He stands at the line, rubbing the ball before throwing it toward the chicken basket. But his aim is off. The ball falls in the basket marked "fish." The contestant lowers his head. The camera cuts to Zack Fox, who wears a knowing look.

Points are tallied after the game, with its multiple questions, is over. The three contestants with the lowest totals stand before the giant screen.

"You three have the lowest totals," Jenna says from the screen. "Why should you stay on *Love Balloon*?"

The first contestant, Bob, a striker, says, "You should keep me on *Love Balloon* because I can bench press three hundred pounds. I can mop the floor with any of these geeks. I can throw a football through a tire seventy-five yards away and I can fix your car."

The second contestant, Deion, a normal guy, says, "You should keep me on the show because my aim was off today. I didn't do a very good job throwing the balls during the challenge. But I know your favorite food is fish, and I know you like reading books better than magazines, and that your favorite time of day is right after the sun sets, and that if you could take a vacation anywhere in the world it would be to New Zealand."

The third contestant, James, also a normal guy, says, "I had bad aim, too. You should keep me on the show because I promise I'll be nice to you if I get to the second season. We'll split the chores and the cooking so both of us have time to do things on our own. And we'll do a lot of things together, too. We'll go for walks in the woods the way you like and pick apples in the fall and drink fresh cider from the press."

Jenna wears a pensive face.

Her screen goes blank.

Zack Fox puts his fingertips to his ear. Repeat viewers have come to notice the almost invisible earpiece nestled there. Almost imperceptibly, he nods.

"Jenna has weighed her options," he says.

The crowd cheers. The phrase has become a cultural phenomenon, appearing on T-shirts and coffee mugs as well as in everyday conversation.

"The contestant who will be going home tonight—who will not have a chance to participate in the *Love Balloon* auction at the end of the season, is . . ."

The camera pans across the contestants' faces.

"Bob."

"Thank you, Bob, for playing *Love Balloon*."

Bob walks to the center of the stage and shakes Zack Fox's hand. He then walks down a dark hallway under the light of a single bulb.

As he departs, his exit speech plays:

"Of course I'm mad. I mean, I have way more to offer than those two scrawny geeks inside. What she needs is a real man. Those dweebs don't fit the bill. I bet neither of them has been inside a gym a day of their lives. Jenna, if you get stuck with one of those two losers, give me a call. I'll show you a real man."

"That's all the time we have for this week," Zack Fox says. "Tune in next week, when nine contestants compete. I'm Zack Fox. From all of us at *Love Balloon*, good night!"

16.

THE LIGHTS BUZZED. CRACKLED. WHITE WALLS. Paneled ceiling. Imagined working there. That buzz all day. Sit quietly. At a desk. Fill out papers. Kids in high school. His classes. This is what they wanted. Sit at a desk to sit at a desk.

Every noise louder. Felt a headache coming behind his eyes. Waiting area. Old magazines. Lady next to him sniffled. Every forty-five seconds. He timed it. Nothing else to do. Sniff, sniff. Not like gunshots where he stopped hearing it, or bells on the door of the garage. Every one worse. In his spine first, then up and down his body.

She got called. Sniffler. Went in. Stephanie, they said. Stood up and sniffled in. Then other things: flipping pages. Chairs against the carpet. Breathing. Music playing. Bad versions of bad songs. No vocals. But he knew them. Did you ever know that you're my hero. Do you know the way to San Jose. Have you ever seen the rain. One after another. When he left one would be stuck in his head. Didn't know which one. Didn't matter. Poor bastards who worked there. Bringing work home with them. Always heard that. Peck. When I get back I'm gonna do customizing and detailing. Great work. Then at the end of the day I'll leave it in the garage. Forget all about that shit. Start drinking.

Not worry about a goddamn thing. Can't wait. These people couldn't. Dancing on the ceiling at work. Then at home. Every day. I bless the rains down in Africa.

Looked at magazines. Heard the songs. Knew every one. Everyone called but him. Some people got there after him, sat down, got called.

Finally: Royal Eggleton.

Same lady. Always looked like someone farted.

Hello, Royal, she said when he stood up. Saw her eyes change. Like oh, him. Great.

Led him through a maze of cubes. Heard the music. Reeling in the years. Always got lost trying to get out. A left, a right. Another. Another. Stopped paying attention. Distracted. Reeling solo. Wasn't bad. Conversations. Some sounded happy. I might have something for you. Have you tried the . . . ? I'd advise you to . . . A right. She sat down at a desk. Remembered the picture. Smiling little girl. Missing front tooth. Cute. She gestured at the chair.

Well, Royal, she said. I'm afraid the news isn't very good. Her face looked pinched. Like she didn't want him there. As you know, construction jobs are very hard to come by.

I know, he said. Didn't worry about it the whole time he was away. Glad. Enough shit to deal with. Came back and got blindsided. Stupid. Should never have listened. But glad he did.

The manufacturing sector has largely been outsourced to foreign soil, eliminating a majority of jobs at mills and factories. We have been doing our best to find work for you, but the longest tenured employees hold their jobs tight. Union regulations.

And I'm afraid the janitorial jobs in the area are the same way. And landscaping. The number of applicants has increased dramatically with the closure of so many mills and factories. While you were gone Northeast Paper closed. That alone added another eight hundred to the pool.

Janitorial. Cleaned shit as punishment. Turd splatter. Got shot at. Almost died. Artillery. Qualified him to clean shit. Or put paper cups in boxes all day.

Isn't there anything else?

In the past, we have placed veterans in call centers. These jobs have moved south. And cameras and surveillance equipment have taken the place of traditional security in many workplaces. It's cheaper to install a high-tech system than it is to hire a staff. This is a shame. With your military background you are perfectly qualified for security.

At least standing with a gun made sense.

Unless you have specific training I'm not sure I'll be able to assist you further at this time.

I used to work on engines. While I was there. Had a lot of experience. Training.

Your profile lists you as artillery.

Well, I was. But there was a shortage. Need. My spare time, I spent on engines.

Engines. I see. What kind of engines?

Trucks, mostly. Some regular. Some diesel.

Diesel.

I've been reading.

Excuse me?

Books. From the library. Foreign. Domestic. Diesel. Gas. Brushing up. I was good at it.

Books from the library.

Plus my experience. Lot of stuff overseas. A lot. I would have gotten more time in if it hadn't been for—

Yes, I know.

—you know, if I hadn't—

Yes, yes. I know. I am aware.

—so maybe you can—

I see. Yes. Um. Of course, yes. Beyond the markets we've previously discussed I may be able to fit you into some kind of mechanical opening. There are a few.

Thank you.

One in Haughton, the other in Hanley.

What about Snooker's?

Excuse me?

Snooker's.

. . .

Garage.

. . .

In Schaferville. Anything there?

Snooker's Garage is not one of our clients.

Friend of mine works there. Artie. Know him?

I don't believe I do, no.

Great guy. Great. Best friends since grade school.

His name does not ring a bell.

Maybe if you saw him.

Maybe, yes. We do not—

Easy to recognize him. Great looking guy. Not that . . . you know—

—of course. We do not —

—I'm just saying is all. Hahahaha.

Yes. We do not work with Snooker's.

Artie works over there.

Yes, as you mentioned. If you have specific establishments in mind, it is a good strategy to visit them yourself and inquire within. We are happy to assist you with your job search, as you know, but feel free to target establishments on your own.

I did. Yesterday. Walked there. Wasn't working.

You should try back again.

I will. I just thought maybe I hadn't told you so I thought I would.

Of course.

Don't know why I didn't think of that before. I guess I was thinking about construction. They promised I'd have work. When I got back. And I didn't. So I didn't think about—

Of course, Royal.

Hard getting back to normal.

Yes.

Didn't want to think about it. You know. About being overseas.

Of course. I do wish you had mentioned it upon your initial screening.

Didn't think of it.

I could have been looking at that sector of the job market for you all this time.

Couldn't.

Yes, of course. So, Royal, if there are any specific garages you think would be conducive to your job search, seek them out specifically and directly. Ask them if they need any help. Become known to them.

Are you saying hang around?

Not necessarily hang around, but be frequent in your check backs. This will establish you as a serious candidate.

Okay.

I will do my part.

Thank you.

Stop by in a few weeks.

I will.

As always I will call if anything opens up.

Thank you.

He got up. Realized he didn't know how to get out.

"Hip to be Square" in the background.

Stuck in the middle. Wasn't sure where he was. Looked for an edge. Find a wall, follow it to the lobby. But there were cubes everywhere. Desks. Couldn't see any way out.

Turned around. Went back.

I'm sorry, I—

I'll escort you out, she said, face fartpinched.

She walked him through the maze to the lobby. "Heaven Is a Place on Earth" came on.

Well, Royal, she said. Good luck. I'll be seeing you.

Thank you.

He watched her walk back to her desk.

Hadn't been to garages. Needed to. But wasn't sure. Skills. He had some. Could learn more. But didn't have many. Probably not enough. Was just starting to understand when it happened. Hopefully Artie would vouch for him. Show him things. Get him up to speed. If there were places that needed help bad they might take him. But that stuff she said. About the economy. Mills closing. Made sense. All the closed stores in Schaferville. Except the beer place. And the cheese shop.

One garage on the way back to his place. What was it called. Couldn't remember. Seemed okay. Looked a little expensive. Good. They'd pay.

Hello there, I'm looking for a job. No. Hello, sir. Unless it was a lady. Like at Artie's. Ma'am? Miss? Madam? Couldn't remember which. Always changed. Maybe just hello. That would work. Hello. I am just back from overseas. No. More. I have just returned from serving our country. Too much. I just got back from Afghanistan where I worked on engines. Good. I'm a war veteran with experience fixing engines. Maybe that was it.

The place was in that strip. Not much of anything there. A few houses. Carpet store. Some trees. Woods. He went there a few times. When he was little. Might as well. Explore. But it was boring. No quarries or hearses or anything. Surprised it wasn't developed yet. Always happened. Buy land, build houses. All looked the same. Matter of time. Then cheese shops would go in. Lots of people with houses. Hopefully two cars each. Need more garages.

She said mechanical. That was good. Didn't realize until now. Not mechanic. Mechanical. Like working on big machines. Factories. Wouldn't be so bad. Handyman. Fix things when they broke. Have to learn them. But he could. Good with his hands. Belts, grease. All made sense to him. Missed that. The grease. Hands clean since he got back.

Passed a little house. Barely big enough for two people to stand in. Java Express, it said. Drive-up coffee. Closed. No shit. Expensive. Snob coffee. Espresso. When he drank coffee, Dunkin' Donuts every time. Only at night. Driving someplace, or back. Mostly Boston. Artie. Back from Sox games. Made him feel nervous. Some of the guys, they drank coffee before patrol. Peck. Long. Donaldson. College Boy. Gotta stay alert, Peck said. Have your senses heightened. He tried it. All he could see was his hands shaking. And the next morning was a headache. Not behind the eyes. Different. Top of his brain. Sharp.

Trees. Woods.

Streetlight down the road. Thought that's where the garage is. Nice place like that would have its own light. Pay well. Let him work on a beater. Fix it up. Maybe on weekends, if there was downtime. Days off. Or he could wait. The walk wasn't so bad.

Did more walking every day, around the common, to the quarry. Leg getting stronger.

The garage. No light yet. Too early. But it looked good. New. All brick. Not old stuff. Brick face. Supposed to look like a garage but nice also. Auto Emporium, it said.

Went in. Same music as the unemployment office. "Land Down Under." Lobby had leather chairs. Big TV. ESPN. Glass table. Magazines. *Men's Health*, *Newsweek*. No one reading them. All on laptops. Tablets. Phones.

Hello, I've just returned from overseas. Where I worked on engines. No, not right. Sounded weird. I worked on engines there. Better. I'm wondering if you have any openings. Close. Maybe job openings. I'm wondering if you have any job openings. That was it. Sounded good.

Woman behind the counter. Old, kinda. Dyed hair. Smiled. Are you here to pick up?

What?

Your car?

Oh. Uh, no. I, uh. I'm wondering if you need help.

Damnit. Stupid.

Uh, if you have any job openings.

Did you see the ad?

Act like you did. That means they're hiring.

I did.

Great. Hang on a sec.

She disappeared.

Holy shit. Good luck. Timing. Whatever. A job. Save money. Get a better place. Someplace warmer.

But wait. No guarantee. Don't get too excited. Might not happen. Probably won't.

She came back. Pad in her hand. Pink. Applications.

Here you go, hon. Do you need a pen?

Yes.

She nodded her head. Mug of them on the counter.

Thanks, he said. Be right back.

Leather chair. Sat. Started application.

Work experience.

Infantry, he wrote. Division and unit. Then: mechanical repair. Specialty: engines. He put his high school job at the mill, too.

At the counter, the woman still there.

All finished, hon?

Yes. I've been having a hard time finding work. Since I got back. From Afghanistan.

You were over there?

He nodded. Yes, ma'am. But I repaired engines.

What kinds?

Diesel. Domestic. Foreign.

She nodded. Some of our guys are going to the new place. We're opening another Auto Emporium in Wilburton. So this might be some easy stuff for you. Oil changes, mufflers. Inspections.

It's tough, he said. You know. Finding work.

I know, hon. Thanks for filling this out. I'll make sure Ahmed gets it. He's the owner.

Okay, thanks.

He's going to take applications and do calls. Hopefully you'll get one. He likes vets. Believes in what you're doing over there.

Good.

If you don't hear back in a week or so, call. Or come by.

What's your name?

Doris.

Okay, he said. Doris. Are you in the phone book?

Hang on, she said. Bent behind the counter. Stood up. Here's a card.

Doris Martineau, it said. Business manager, Auto Emporium. Give me a call. She looked at the application. Royal?

Roy.

She took a pen and wrote "Roy" at the top.

Roy. No guarantees. But we'll do what we can. Sound good?

Yes, ma'am. Thank you.

One last thing. Where did you see the ad?

If I say the Internet that sounds safe. Unless they don't use it. They must. No one uses newspapers.

I can't remember where.

We've got a lot of ads out.

Sorry.

She laughed. Sounded like a dog barking. That's okay, hon. Anyway, you have a great day, 'kay?

I will, he said. Thank you.

Door rang as he left. Went good. Really good. Even though he screwed up the beginning. That question. Picking up. Thought she was talking about weed. Artie. Always saying "I've got to pick up a pizza" on the phone instead of weed. Safer that way. Code. In case people were listening. Never know who's on the other end, he said. Tripped him up. But she was nice. Seemed to like him. Wrote his name on the top of the application. That was good.

Song in his head. Must've heard it in the office. Or the garage. "I Saw the Sign."

17.

Today Mom was home after school.

She said Dixon, we need to talk.

I was like oh no.

Was it the bike? The iPad? The fireworks? School? Mary?

Did she find this thing and listen to it?

She said Don is being redeployed.

I put my head down because I felt myself smiling.

She said I know. It's hard. But we'll have to get by.

Once I stopped smiling so much I asked when. She said six weeks. He won't be able to see your brother play if they make it to the finals.

I can't believe it.

I still wanna leave, but this is good. If I get drunk again he won't give me shit if I puke.

At first I thought maybe he'll get shot. But if he did Mom would just find another guy. He's not the worst one.

I asked for how long. She said she didn't know yet.

Then I asked if there would be a party or something before he left. She said no, he doesn't want anything like that. Just to go to games. Then she said did he talk to you about that? I said yeah.

The bruise has been changing color. Now it's this weird blue. Maybe I would've showed it to her if she didn't tell me about him going back. I don't know. Probably not.

She said what were you thinking? and I said I don't know, I was just having fun. She said you made a fool of yourself. I was like I know, but I'll never do it again. And I won't. At least until he leaves.

She did the whole thing about hurting Ross's chances and Nebraska and all the stuff Don said and I was like okay, I know, and she stopped. Thank God. I thought she was gonna say I had a problem and blah blah blah.

Then she went I almost forgot to tell you. You got a message while you were at school. Someone from a burger place. I said Gary? And she said do you know him? I told her I was applying for jobs. She said well, that's good. What for? I shrugged and said something about helping out and she said well, that's great. When your brother is in school things will be a little easier. Until then I think a little extra money will be a big help.

I called the number she wrote down and asked for Gary. He said can you come over tomorrow for an interview? I said I could. After school.

* * *

Maybe I shoulda kept some of that stuff. Like the iPad. That thing seemed pretty cool. But I don't even have a phone. Don would see it and know. And I don't want him pissed off. Especially now.

* * *

At school today Merrill gave a test. Of course I didn't read the book.

I thought about Don being pissed off before he leaves. So I went to Merrill after class and told him my mom's boyfriend is being redeployed and things are rough at home. He looked surprised when I came over to talk to him. He said well, it's good to know. And what can I do to help? I told him I wanted to get back on track. He asked if I had been doing the reading and I said not really. He told me to get caught up and I could take the test again. Then he asked if I have the book. I do. It's in my locker somewhere.

* * *

I talked to Trombley, too. Same story. He gave me some worksheets and said if you can do all the problems here you should do well on the tests.

I just need to keep them all off my back until Don leaves.

I need to find my books. They're in my locker someplace. Unless someone stole them. Which I doubt. Who'd want to steal a bunch of books?

* * *

Gary says I can start as soon as possible. I'm doing weekends, so I have to miss games. I think this week is away. I don't know if those guys go. Probably. It's against Enoch. I bet they drive there. I'll ask Mary. If I don't get to see her this weekend maybe we can go back up to the hearse next week. I hope so.

I start at training wage, then minimum wage. He said I'd get raises based on my performance.

It's a bunch of guys working there. The only lady is old. Like grandma old.

* * *

I started reading that book. It's weird. It doesn't start at the beginning.

* * *

Don came in when I was reading. He said what are you doing? and I said school stuff. I should've closed my door like usual. He came in and sat next to me on my bed. I was like what the hell is this?

He said whatcha reading? and I said a book for school. He said that's about war. I was like yeah. He said I'm getting redeployed, you know, and I said yeah, Mom told me. He said it's getting dangerous over there. I said well, be careful.

I got up and went to my bag and pretended to look for something. I put all the books and stuff in there after school, which was stupid, because I had to carry them all the way to Burger Hut. I could feel his eyes on me.

Then the front door opened. Mom.

He got up and went to talk to her. And shut the door behind him.

* * *

The grandmother lady showed me around Burger Hut all day. Judy, her name is. She's nice. And she swears like a rapper.

There's a fry station, which I'm going to work a lot at first, and grill, and sandwich, and the register, and two drive-through windows. One takes the money and one delivers the food. She says working delivery is best. You don't have to talk to so many people and it's not hot.

I asked her how long she's been working here and she said two years.

Everything's on a buzzer. She said after a while I'll hear it in my sleep. It tells you when to stop and start. We did fries for a while, then orders. It's not hard. Just fast. She said everyone should get their food in three minutes. Sometimes the company gives awards for being the fastest. She won everything, so she almost didn't get to be assistant manager. She started laughing and said don't get too good at what you do, honey, because you might get stuck doing it forever. When she laughs she sounds like she's gonna hack up a lung.

It's weird. There's her and these old guys Jack and Herbert. They're like grandpas. Then there's people my age. I don't know any of them except this one guy, Dalton, and I don't really know him. I just recognize him from school. He's one of like three black guys in town. He looks like he's gonna hit his head on something, he's so tall. He plays basketball. Then there's this short fat kid I've seen around before. He doesn't hang out with the geeks, but he still kinda looks scared every time I get near him, so maybe he does hang out with them or I stole his lunch money or something. Or maybe he was there that time I crashed a fat kid convention, hahaha.

It goes by quick. Judy said it's not bad except for working cashier. I'll have to train there next. She said most people who eat at the Burger Hut don't know what they want and have lots of questions even though they get lunch there every day. I got this big packet of menu descriptions I have to study to learn all the ingredients, so that should help.

We all take turns on the stations, I guess. She said some people like cashier, like Paul. He might trade sections, as long as Gary isn't there. She told me Gary mostly works nights.

* * *

In class Merrill was explaining the title of the book. The only way to get out of the trap is to stay in the trap. *Catch-22*. I said like living in a town where the only way to get out is to save a bunch of money but the only way to get money is to work a job you can't leave that doesn't pay. He kinda looked surprised but nodded and said very good, Dixon.

* * *

I saw Mary after school. She asked if I wanted to hang out this weekend. Big game at Enoch. We like to go and make noise. And you're so funny at games.

I told her I couldn't go.

She looked all sad and said why not?

I told her I had to train at the Burger Hut.

She laughed.

I was like what? and she said I can't believe you decided to work there. I said well, I did. I need money if I'm gonna move out. She said so, do you wanna hang out next weekend? I said any day I have off and she smiled and said okay, find me after class and tell me.

Then she said maybe next weekend.

I was like I think I'll have to work, and she started laughing again and said there's a reason why it's all boys and old people who work there. Even I know, and I'm new. Wait and see.

* * *

After school Mom was home. So were Don and Ross. We had to clean the house. Recruiters are coming. Don said Alabama and Oklahoma. Ross didn't seem like he cared that much. He says those schools are too hot. Don was like you have to get all your ducks in a row in case something doesn't work out.

Mom said she wanted me around but I said I couldn't. Don said what are you talking about? and I was like I'm training at Burger Hut. Ross started laughing at me and I was like shut up. Don said don't talk to your brother like that and I said he was laughing at me. It went back and forth and then Mom said that's enough. Then she said she was happy everything worked out with the job. Ross was all good luck and I was like what do you mean? Ross said that guy is a perv. Don got all red and said I have known Gary Stites for years. He's a good man. Ross said yeah, a good man who messes around with his staff. Don said that's not true and Ross started laughing. Don didn't tell him to shut up.

Neither did Mom. She just said you'll miss dinner. We might go out with the recruiters. To the Cowboy or someplace like that. Ross said maybe we'll swing by the Hut and get a few Downtown Deluxes. I said don't be a dick and of course Don was like don't talk to your brother like that, again. So I was all whatever, Don, and left.

It was too dark to go anywhere but the L'il Bee. There wasn't anyone I knew around. I was hoping Mary would be there. I should ask where she lives.

I keep thinking about what she said at school. And Ross. About that guy being a perv. I don't give a shit. I wanna save some money. Get out of here.

18.

BIKING WAS UNCOMFORTABLE, BUT ZACHARIAH STILL thought of it as the best way to lose weight. And riding his bike made him feel bold; he knew, despite his size, that he was still faster on two wheels than anyone was on foot.

He went on the Patch Bike Challenge.

The kids at soccer practice had talked about the place in the woods where the older, high school types went to drink beer and smoke cigarettes and make out: no middle schoolers allowed. Sal the goalie knew a kid who had a brother whose friend had been beaten up by kids who hung out there; Sal's friend's brother's friend simply dared to walk the trails behind the L'il Bee and had landed in the hospital with a broken arm.

Yet the Patch was magnetic despite its potential dangers. For one, there was an abandoned hearse out there. Zachariah had heard about it for years. He was pleased to discover, after his initial visit, that it lived up to its lofty reputation. Layers of graffiti which struck him as archeological in nature, applied and reapplied by generations of high schoolers, giant spouting penises among the more specific messages boasting JOHN G. CRUSHED BEERS and TOM BLEW A WAD HERE 7/98 and MARIANNE GIVES GREAT HEAD and, simply, Pussy. It was fascinating stuff—evidence that the hearse, with its patina of broken glass and bottle caps, rusty springs bursting from tears in the seats, which looked and felt like real leather, had been an institution for years. Zachariah wanted to ask his dad about it—how it had gotten there, and when—but feared doing so would incur a beating, reminding Paul Tietz of the good times he'd had prior to Zachariah's accidental arrival, or, alternately, some ill-fated visit. He didn't know who else he could ask and hadn't found any information about it online.

There were the quarries out there, too. On his initial visit he heard them well in advance of seeing them—the echoes of splashes and yells hit him even before his arrival at the long, steady hill leading to the path spilling onto the spray-painted granite rim. He had been spooked by the sounds and stopped his ascent. Stupid. The only way to get to the top on his bike was with a full head of steam.

His next visit was quiet. No jumpers. Nobody at all. He could explore.

At the far end of the quarry, near a stubby granite jut named Cock, was a path. He walked it with his bike, winding past unrecognizable tall plants.

With each passing minute, Zachariah wondered if he was on a path to nowhere. At some point he'd have to turn around. He didn't want to get stuck in the woods after dark.

Then he saw a ring of unfinished houses in the distance.

This was the Mayers Road development, he knew—the boundary his father had set for his biking, past the trailer park. He remembered his dad talking about a rich developer—Paul called him a Masshole—thinking that nice houses would be a fine addition to Armbrister. The Masshole poured foundations and began construction on twenty-three houses.

Construction stopped after one mill closed and another laid off half of its employees. Paul had been nervous throughout, which meant he'd been drinking more, which in turn meant that Zachariah had been hit more. The layoffs coincided with soccer season, so Zachariah had told his father about fictional practices. He feared the lies would come back to haunt him—that Paul might call the coach, or bump into Jim's parents—but nothing, thankfully, had come of them.

His dad, job eventually secured, laughed at the developer's stupidity.

"There's not enough money in this town," he said one night over dinner, "for some Masshole to make a bunch off of us. Or to move in more of those Massholes."

The development had remained unfinished since. It reminded Zachariah of the hearse and the quarry. Cigarette butts ringed the houses, broken bottles. He was surprised none of the houses were spray-painted. He had heard someone tried to set one on fire.

If he got caught out here, kids nearby might beat him up, or give him titty twisters, but it wouldn't be as bad as getting hit by his dad's sock. Besides, he liked the rush he felt when visiting dangerous places. The feeling was the same as when he stopped a chest-thumping striker from scoring a goal.

Maybe if he went into the development he could use his powers to keep him safe. And the rush would be bigger than visiting either the quarry or the hearse.

While he was kneading dough, the idea of taking the road to the development—called Whispering Pines—popped into his head, fully formed. He was surprised, but not entirely—he often had ideas while making bread. He could circumvent biking the steep quarry hill entirely if he took the roads. He knew he wasn't supposed to bike so far, but the idea gave him a jolt.

After school he gingerly picked his way through the exiting crowd—and past Dixon's locker, just a few steps from the front door, past the ancient security guard who stood there grinning before and after school—to the bike rack, intent on heading just past Mayers to the development.

He had just entered Whispering Pines when he heard it.

The explosion—what else could he call it?—was loud, but still somehow muffled.

He almost fell off his bike. Shaking, he piloted it to the nearest house and hid behind it.

The noise had come from inside one of the houses. He had no way of telling which.

Glass littered the ground, cigarette butts, strange square wrappers. Rust streaks stretched like shadows from nailed walls.

He smelled burning.

Someone was in one. Setting it on fire?

He remounted his bike and began to push off when he heard another, louder explosion.

Across the way, a bike leaned against a house's wall.

Whoever was making the noise owned that bike.

He could get away fast if he needed to. And he didn't think that whoever was inside would direct something at him—they'd get in trouble, even arrested, if he got hurt.

The noises were loud. But Zachariah felt the rush coming on.

He pedaled to the side of the building opposite the leaning bike. The windows there were at eye level. Zachariah thought the Masshole was lucky—if he had installed glass, it would have been broken by now.

The sun shone into the unfinished house in such a way that everything inside glowed orange—including Dixon Dove, who stood in the middle of the room with a paper bag at her feet. The outline of her body was illuminated. Zachariah thought she looked beautiful like that. He felt himself getting hard.

She fiddled with something he couldn't make out.

An explosion echoed throughout the empty house.

He couldn't believe how loud it was, or how smoky. He ducked down, trying not to gasp or cough as he breathed clean air.

When he looked again, Dixon Dove did not seem impressed, mumbling to herself. He couldn't distinguish words, but what he could see of her face in profile through the smoke was not excited.

The smell hit him after the sound and smoke did. He understood.

When she titty twisted him she had that smell. Like the one hanging in the air. Gunpowder. From setting off fireworks in empty houses. And the char of burnt wood.

It was probably her who tried to burn one down.

Zachariah felt his eyes widen.

I have to get out of here, he thought. Right now. She's the one. If she knows I saw her it won't just be titty twisters. I have to get away.

Wait, he thought.

He peeked back inside. She was squatting, hands rustling inside the paper bag.

I need to get out of here right now.

He took another look. The bag was on the floor, and she was standing again, with something in her hand.

He mounted his bike and pedaled as fast as he could. He was four houses down when he heard the next muffled explosion.

19.

Wednesday. Artie working. Wanted to talk to him. And Auto Emporium.

And say hello. Hadn't since the Sox game. Too embarrassed. The calls. Should have picked up. Said sorry, man. Listen, it's tough. Nothing personal. Something. Artie would understand. Always had. All the dumb high school shit. Not jumping. Trying honors. Never gave him shit. Could've. Like kids in his classes. Before he tried college prep. Saying he was too good for them. Wanted to say hey, I hate this shit. My great-aunt. She pays the bills. But that would remind everyone. The mom thing had gone away. Really bad for a while. Then she died. Couldn't believe it. How sad he was. Didn't like her. They saw. Maybe in the paper. Or on him. Had to put his shoulders back. Sorry about your mom. Now I won't be able to get a blo—Hit them. In the face. Hurt his hand. Felt good. Principal's office. What am I supposed to do with you? You've suffered this tragedy and you're acting out. He said I don't care. And he didn't. Detention, suspension. Do whatever you want. They're saying stuff about my mom. My dead mom. Calling her a whore. I'm not gonna take it. If I do they'll never stop. Royal, I—Roy said come on, you know. You must.

The principal stood up. Held his arm to the door. Go ahead. Go.

Never said anything when Artie was there. He could fight. Saw him once. At a party. Some guy grabbed Christa's ass. Artie tapped him on the shoulder. Dropped him. One punch. The guy's friend came over. Swung. Artie ducked. Hit him in the stomach. Kneed him in the face. Blood everywhere. Broke his nose. Kicked him on the ground. Looked around. Anyone else? Come on, Artie said to her. And him. Let's go. This party's a bunch of fucking homos.

Second walk to the garage was easier. Leg feeling stronger. Did it once before. Familiar. Still too long. A bike, maybe. Or a beater. Kept thinking about that. Buying a car. Couldn't drive. Scared. Too much. But wanted to. Maybe someday. Good job, good pay. Good apartment. Not think of the past all the time. Be in the now. Not worry. Get used to it. Sarge before they went. Let me tell you something. Every now and then I am sent a no-hope fuckup and I manage to turn him around before he hurts somebody. You were one of those fuckups, Eggleton. You might just make it.

Couldn't tell that to Auto Emporium. Maybe to Artie. His garage. Listen, man. I can learn anything. I got through basic. I got through the fucking desert. School. Graduated. Barely. Started failing classes. Hard to care. Even with Auntie Blake there. Royal, you need to think of your future. Hard to. Didn't want college. Even if he did, no money. Auntie Blake told him. If you do well enough, you may qualify for loans and grants. She talked about Plymouth, Durham, Keene. Never went to those towns. Concord a few times. On the way to Boston, mostly. But Artie. He met a girl from Concord. Always met girls. Didn't know how. Maybe the Internet. Never talked about it. Went down with him. Double date. Got one for you, my man. Horsey girl. Artie's girl's friend. She didn't like him. Walked around with her anyway. Artie and the girl in the car. Downtown at night.

Capital building. Gold dome. Car steamed up when they walked by. Laps around downtown. Not saying anything. Finally the car windows opened. They drove back. More than two hours. Any luck?

Wouldn't go even if he had the grades. Wouldn't go now that he had the GI Bill. Didn't know anyone who went. Except Auntie Blake. Look where she got: the same place as him. Nowhere Armbrister. No thanks. But he took her classes. She told him without telling him. She was like that. Liked the Army better. Told you what they wanted. You did it. Easy. Like working at a garage. Fix this.

Through downtown. Past the cheese shop. Beer place. Wished they had a bar instead. Have one after he saw Artie. Or lunch break. Come on man, I know a place. They could have beers. At a bar. Hadn't been with him yet. That time at Fenway was their first legal one. And he ruined it. AC/DC.

Check still hadn't come. He'd call. Wait another day. Hated it. Weren't people at the other end. Computers. Taking jobs. Made no sense. Asking which department. Speak clearly into the phone. Didn't understand no matter what. He was an American war veteran. Wanted to talk to an American. Not a computer. Took hours. No check.

Still had his quarters. Decided to get a beer last night, play a few games. Check would arrive soon. Ordered at the bar. Some kid came in. College. White hat. Asked Patterson if anyone played pool. She looked at Roy for a second. Didn't blow his cover, say this guy here. Instead, she said, loud, does anyone here play pool? Maybe she wasn't so bad. Could've said oh, Roy's here all the time. Didn't. Stood there at the bar. Played dumb. No one answered. Patterson finished pulling his Venerable. The kid stepped away. Well, Roy said. If no one else will I'll play with you.

Played lefty. Did okay. The kid was good, though. Beat him. Then again. Roy tried to win. Hard. Missed a few. Wasn't faking.

It helped. He knew it. Good players saw acting. He never acted. Wanted to beat everyone lefty. But happy to switch.

The kid said twenty bucks says I get the next game.

I only have fifteen, Roy said. Beer, games. A tip. But I have more in the ATM. Which was a lie. Which the kid would never know.

That's fine, the kid said. Tell you what. I'll put in twenty for your fifteen. Make things more fair. Sound good?

Roy nodded. Stupid kid. Lefty again. Too early to switch. Wanted it bad. Almost had him. Lost by one ball. Fucking fuck, he said. One fucking ball. And I'm out of money. Good job. Tell you what, the kid said. Best of three.

Roy said I don't know. How much a game?

Fifty a game, Roy said.

The kid said sure.

Roy broke. Still lefty. Lost by two balls. Kid said fifty bucks. On top of the fifteen you owe me.

I'll pay at the end. You can come to the ATM with me.

Last game, the kid said. Broke.

Roy said best of five.

Wanna bet?

Sure, Roy said. Double down. Hundred a game.

And the kid bit.

They shook on it.

He switched hands.

Kid knew right away. Cords stuck out of his neck.

Didn't even give him a shot.

One, two, three.

Hundred a game. Minus what I owe you. Pay up.

Had it. In his wallet. Roy didn't feel bad. Kid wouldn't miss it.

Let me buy you a beer.

The kid said I don't want your fucking beer. You hustled me.

Come by any time. Maybe I'll beat you lefty, too.

The kid's jaw clenched. Didn't say anything. Put on his coat. Left.

He'd tell Artie the story. Buy him a beer. Great time. Except there was nowhere but the beer supply store.

The beep, the bells on the door tinkled when he went inside.

Same lady as before at the counter. Hey, hon, she said. You back for Artie?

Yes, ma'am. Is he around?

She opened the door behind the counter and yelled ARTIE, SOMEONE HERE FOR YOU into the garage.

He'll be right over, she said.

Artie walked into the office wiping his hands on a rag. Grease. Roy, he said. Hey. Good to see you. What are you doing here?

Wanna get some lunch?

I'm in the middle of something, he said. How'd you get here, anyway?

Walked.

From Armbrister?

Isn't so bad, he said. Did it the other day, too.

The other day?

Oh, hon, I musta forgot to tell you your friend came by to see you.

So you came twice.

He nodded.

Sheila, I'm gonna take a few minutes to talk to my friend here. Have you met? Sheila, Roy; Roy, Sheila. She stuck out a chubby hand. He shook.

Hello.

Nice to meet you, Roy, she said. Take a few minutes to see your friend. Must be important for you to walk all the way out here. Twice.

Artie patted his chest. Looking for something. He said come outside, man. Walked out. Around the side, away from downtown. Kept patting. Pulled a lighter out from his coveralls. Cigarettes. Cold out here. Lit one up.

You smoke?

Yeah, I started. I'm breathing fumes all day anyway. Figured I might as well enjoy it.

Breathing fumes. Everything he did overseas was outside. Under a tent. In the open. Something. Never inside like Artie. Like Auto Emporium. Maybe he'd smoke. Doubted it. Expensive. Tried once. At a party. High school. Puked. No one saw.

I have a job lead, he said.

That's great! Where?

Auto Emporium.

The muffler place?

Yeah.

That's good work. Entry level.

What do you mean?

Oil changes, mufflers. Learn some stuff. Get a better job later.

I worked on trucks overseas

But you were infantry. It's hard to get a job unless you specialized.

How do you know?

Because I tried to get you in.

You did?

I thought it would be fun to work together. But Sheila, she said no. You have to get some experience first. It'd take too much time to show you everything. Cars and trucks are different, you know?

I guess.

Is that why you came?

Yeah. To ask about a job.

I never told you, man. I thought you'd get bummed out.

No, that's cool.

Is that why you came the other time, too?

Yeah.

Running out of money?

Tired of sitting around all the time. Got nothing to do.

You're living the life, man. Must be nice.

Boring. No friends. Don't know anyone. All I do is play pool. Listen to games. Walk around.

How's your leg?

Good. Better. I go to the library sometimes.

You reading?

Hard to concentrate. I look at manuals.

Manuals?

How to fix cars.

You've gotta get an interview, man. Ace it. Then we'll see what happens.

I'll try.

I think Sheila knows the guy. Achnad, something like that.

Ahmed.

Right.

Threw his butt down. Ground it under his boot heel. Let's go, man.

Where?

Inside. We'll talk to Sheila.

She was at the counter still. Remember I was talking to you about my friend who just got back? From Afghanistan? This is him. Roy Eggleton.

She put both hands on the counter. Well. I thank you for your service, and your country thanks you, too. Putting your life on the line for freedom.

He didn't know what to say. Felt weird. But good.

Roy has a lead at Auto Emporium.

They're expanding, she said. Opening a new one. Good place. Fast. Nice. She laughed. Nicer than this place.

Roy's been having a hard time finding work, Artie said. He worked on some trucks over there but didn't specialize.

It's tough out there, Sheila said. Maybe I can give Ahmed a call. See if that helps.

That would be great, he said.

If you get some time in a place like that under your belt you can do other things.

Yes, ma'am.

What have you been doing?

What?

Since you got back.

Oh. Um, looking for work.

What about money?

I get a little check.

Her head moved up and down. Hon, you look fine.

My leg. Bad enough to get sent back.

You're a lucky guy.

I guess, he said.

Luckier than Peck. He didn't get to live in a shitty apartment with no insulation. He didn't get to walk around with a limp. Peck didn't get to play pool because he had nothing else to do. Or walk eight miles each way to talk to his only friend. But it beat being dead. He thought. Maybe being dead was better.

Maybe Peck was in heaven having a great time playing the harp. Sitting on a cloud. If dead was better and no one alive knew they'd laugh when he got there. To heaven. He thought he might go there. Wasn't sure about God anymore after what he saw over there—did—but hopefully if there was one there was a free war pass like, okay, we understand you had to do some fucked up shit when you went over and it's what you did after that really counts. And before, too. After and before. Remembered some class— English it must've been—teacher talking about hell. Sounded bad. All the suicides went there. And the people who didn't worship God but were good people. Greeks. Maybe that was everyone who went to war.

Beats the alternative.

It does.

Well, Artie said.

You have to get back to work.

I do. Good to see you, though.

You too.

We should hang out.

Yeah. I'm sorry man after the game and the parking lot I just—

No worries, man. Good to see you again.

Nice to meet you again, Roy, Sheila said. I'll give Ahmed a call.

Thanks.

20.

TODAY AT WORK DALTON FIGURED IT out. He said did I hear Judy call you Dixon Dove? When I said yeah, he was like does that make Ross Dove your brother? I said yeah again, and he was like man, your brother is famous! I said whatever, but he kept saying that Ross is the best athlete in Armbrister sports history.

We were putting burgers together. He wanted to know where Ross is going to play. I told him he hasn't decided yet. Dalton started naming all these schools and one of them was Nebraska, so I told him about the recruiters. He said pros go there. And that everyone is rooting for Ross. I was like what? and he said yeah, everyone in town hopes he gets out.

He doesn't know Ross at all, but he feels like he knows him. Weird.

Dalton said he might be one of the best basketball players in Armbrister and look where it got him. He said hopefully I can get into some school and get out of town after I graduate. Even down to Durham would be cool. Get a degree, at least, not be stuck putting burgers together. But the pros? Never happen. Million to one. But everyone thinks your brother can go.

I thought about that the whole shift.

If I do get out of here—no, when I get out of here, I have to think about it like that, when—what am I gonna do? Go somewhere else and do the same thing. Flip burgers.

For me, getting out is going someplace new.

If Ross goes pro, he's set. If he doesn't, he'll still have a degree. The only way I can go to college will be by having enough money. If you have it, you can get out, but you don't need to.

* * *

I hit the parking lot after work.

I found a knife. It was in this jacked-up pickup covered with mud. I could've gotten a shotgun out of there if I wanted it.

The knife rules. It folds. Huge blade. The handles are covered with red jewels, and there's a little picture of an old car in the middle of the handle. I can carry it no problem.

No phones or iPads or anything like that. Just some wallets. No credit cards after what Ding told me. Just cash. About fifty bucks.

I might do just cash from now on, unless there's something too good to pass up, like an iPad. But that'll never happen again.

* * *

It was getting dark but I had a feeling, so I went up to the quarry and everyone was there.

I snuck up there and tried to sound like a cop when I heard everybody. I said all right, you kids, you're all under arrest. Everyone looked like they were going to shit themselves. I started laughing and they called me an asshole. Pretty funny.

Steve was like hey, working girl, how's the Burger Hut treating you? I said okay. Earl wanted to know if the old perv had grabbed my tits. I said not yet and everyone thought that was funny. Even Mary. I guess I was hoping she'd be up there by herself. I mean, I knew she wouldn't be, because it was almost dark, but you know.

I told them I hadn't seen him since the first day, when he interviewed me. I had one training shift left, and it was Judy's day off so I'd work with him then. Kelly said oh, Judy. I guess she used to work there. He was always trying to cop a feel off her. Her tits are way bigger than mine.

I asked her why he always did that and she said because he's a fucking perv and everyone laughed. I was like no, did you get more shifts or something?

She said what, are you gonna let him grab your tits? Everyone kinda looked at me. So I pulled the knife out and said he can grab this. They all started laughing again. Mary said did you always have that? and I was like you know.

Steve said it's too bad you have to miss the game this weekend. I said yeah, I know. I'm doing my last training shift, then my first real one. Earl told me I'd be making the big bucks. Steve said nah, you'll quit by the end of the week. I was like whatever. He said no, seriously. We'll see you for the game next Friday.

Everyone passed a flask so I took some pulls. Then Steve lit a joint and passed that, too, so I hit it. We didn't really talk about anything. I mean, we talked the whole time, but for me it was like I was listening to myself talk without hearing what I was saying. School and stuff. I went and sat next to Mary. It was getting pretty dark but I could feel her looking at me. It was a little weird, I think because we were there with people.

By the time the flask was empty it was dark. We all started walking home. It was hard because there was no moon and hardly any light so we had to look up and find the hole in the tree line and follow that. Mary said hey and I took her hand. She was cool with that but when I tried to kiss her she said no, someone might see. I was like it's dark. She said when are you working next week?

and I said I wasn't sure because the schedule hasn't been made yet. She said let me know and squeezed my hand.

* * *

When I got home I didn't hear anyone around. I went to the fridge and Ross came in and said you little bitch. I was like what? He said you know what. I said no and he hit me across the face. Not that hard—his hand was open. He said I can smell it on you. You're pinching off my stash. I was like no, I was at the quarry.

He said with who? and I told him Steve and Earl and Kelly and Mary and Arnold. He kinda grunted and was like bullshit, you pinched.

I was like do you have any whiskey? I knew he didn't have any, since the last time I was in his room, at least. He said no. So I blew in his face.

I said there. You believe me now?

He said you pinched. I was like I didn't. I smoked Steve's shit. Seriously.

He said sorry I hit you.

I said you're an asshole.

Then he asked me how long I've been smoking. I told him since I started hanging out with those guys. He said Steve is a dealer. I said yeah, I figured. He asked if I ever bought and I said no, I just smoke what they pass.

He looked at me for a minute and was like what about Ding?

I said what about him? He goes you ever buy from him? I said no. I never buy. Ross goes what about those fireworks? I said how'd you know about that? He kinda smiled. He was like come on, Dixon, everyone knows you're into blowing stuff up.

I was kinda surprised by that.

I told Ross I got the fireworks from Ding. He said what do you do to get them? I said I give him shit from cars. He looked surprised. I said I find stuff in cars and trade it for fireworks. Or used to. Now I'm saving money.

Then he goes if you're not pinching my stash it's either Mom or Don. I was like you smoke a lot. He said no, seriously. I said get a new hiding place and he said I move it all the time but it keeps getting smaller. I thought it was you.

I told him it wasn't.

I said Mom works too much for that.

He said it must be Don.

He's probably stressed about going back. But pinching sucks.

Hopefully he smokes so much he can't hit me any more.

I asked Ross what he was gonna do. He said what can I do? Keep trying to hide it. Maybe get a lock for my door. Or a safe. But then if I do that Mom will ask what I have to hide. I said say it's to keep me out. He said it won't matter.

So now I'm worried about my stashes. About this.

I'm going to put the tape in a different place than the recorder.

And I shouldn't bring anything home. Just cash. And I'll hide it in a bunch of places.

21.

ZACHARIAH WALKED TOWARD THE BATHROOM, JAR of cold cream in his hand. His dad yelled down the hall.

"Let's go!"

"I want to take my paint off," he yelled back. He regretted doing so immediately. Stupid. Talking back to his dad.

"Get your ass out here!"

Zachariah ran down the hall. He knew his dad's moods started with the same tone of voice he'd heard while entering the bathroom. They didn't always end with the sock. Usually. But not always.

I don't want Dad to beat me up.

Then: *I just used my powers.* They came out, seemingly, of their own accord—he didn't mean to use them. They were like a reflex. A sneeze.

There must've been times he forgot to use them because he was scared. Or because he used them incorrectly: *Oh, no, she's gonna beat me up!* He needed to train himself to use them at the right times, to keep himself safe. Maybe he could practice by kicking a soccer ball against the wall, toward his nuts—the Use Powers Challenge.

"We're going downtown before everyone else does," Paul said from the sink, voice steady. Zachariah knew he was putting meat under the running faucet to thaw while they were gone. "Got that?"

"Yessir," Zachariah said. He tried not to grin.

"You can take your paint off later."

"Okay," Zachariah said, "I will."

"Put on a shirt, if you want."

Zachariah put on a shirt and jacket.

Above all else, Paul Tietz loved Armbrister blowouts. When the scrubs hit the field, his fandom reached dizzying heights: he knew the names of the second- and third-stringers and over-cheered their routine plays and hits. His enthusiasm was inevitably contagious: given a name, the rest of the crowd had something to latch onto.

The third to last game of the season, a rare Saturday afternoon occasion, was such a blowout: Haughton's small pool of students assured their team also-ran status every year, more so than Enoch, whose team Armbrister had beaten soundly on the road the week before. Fahey connected for touchdowns with four different receivers in the first quarter alone, rendering the second half moot.

Replacements took the field as the marching band resumed its post at the foot of the bleachers. Zachariah shivered, looking for Dixon Dove. He hadn't seen her at the Enoch game the week before—did she go to away games? He thought she'd be leading cheers now that Armbrister was back at home, but she was, mercifully, nowhere to be found. Neither was her brother. Zachariah looked for him all game, anticipating Dixon Dove to appear after Ross made plays, but he wasn't on the field.

Paul Tietz's celebratory mood extended to grilling. Zachariah welcomed the opportunity not to cook for an evening, much as he loved it. "I'll drop you off at L'il Bee while I go across the street," his dad said.

Go across the street was Paul's euphemism for *buy a case of beer*. Zachariah was grateful his father hadn't brought his flask to the game that day—if he had, Zachariah's earlier protest about the body paint might've yielded a fresh beating. But Paul had come home from his mill shift the night before and drank the beer remaining in the fridge. He was snoring in front of the TV set by eight, which Zachariah knew meant he'd be hungover and wouldn't start drinking until midafternoon Saturday, postgame.

They got in the car and drove to the L'il Bee. Traffic was negligible.

Paul pulled into the L'il Bee parking lot.

"Do you know what kind of barbecue sauce?"

"Slow Bull," Zachariah said.

"Good." Paul fished around in his pocket. "Here's ten bucks. That should do it. Buy yourself something. I want some change back, though."

"Okay," Zachariah said. He couldn't remember the last time his dad had told him to buy something for himself. Before his weight gain, probably. The football team needed more blowout wins.

"I'll be right back," Paul said as Zachariah closed the car door. His dad pulled out of the parking lot.

A buzzer announced Zachariah's arrival as he pushed open the L'il Bee's door. He recognized the guy behind the counter, who looked up briefly from whatever he was writing in and smiled.

The only two things Zachariah ever shopped for at L'il Bee were barbecue sauce and hamburger rolls. He was happy to find the sauce shelf well-stocked—a different brand, or, worse, none at all, might push his dad away from remembering blowouts past and into a bad mood.

Find Slow Bull Challenge complete, he stood surveying the candy racks before selecting a bag of spicy gumdrops.

The guy behind the counter had been working on a book of word searches, Zachariah saw as he waited to pay.

"No rolls today?"

"No sir," Zachariah said, placing the sauce and the candy on the counter. "Just this stuff."

"A blowout, I hear."

Sometimes the guy asked Zachariah how school was going or talked about the weather—they never talked about football. How did he know Zachariah had been to the game?

He chuckled as he pushed register buttons. "Team colors," he said.

Duh. Of course.

"You looked confused," the guy said. "Six and a quarter."

Zachariah handed him the ten.

"Need a bag?"

"No thank you," Zachariah said as the guy handed back change.

"See you next time," the guy said.

Zachariah said bye and exited the L'il Bee, the door announcing his departure.

The smell of car exhaust and cigarette smoke was strong outside.

He'd gone in and looked around all painted up. Because he'd been thinking about his powers he'd forgot about his colors.

Zachariah opened his bag of gumdrops and selected a green one. It had been a while since he'd eaten candy. But the smoke and car exhaust were so strong he almost couldn't eat.

He'd seen a red gumdrop underneath the green one. Red was his favorite.

It might be a few minutes. Sometimes his dad saw friends at the liquor store. Especially on game days. Zachariah remembered sitting in the car once for close to half an hour, hoping no one would see him, painted, while his dad stood inside talking about the state championship.

"TIETZ."

Zachariah knew the voice.

His mind went loose with fright.

Dixon Dove emerged from around the corner. The stink of cigarettes enveloped her, though Zachariah could not smell the explosive aroma that usually accompanied her appearance.

"School colors," she said, smirking.

Zachariah said nothing. He felt himself trembling.

"You go to all the games, Tietz?" She put a hand on one of his boobs. He recognized alcohol under the cigarette smell. Both were on her breath. He could feel it on his face when she talked. There were other smells around her, too, that he didn't recognize—girl smells, maybe, though he didn't remember them from his mom. Maybe they were teenage girl smells.

Her eyes had a look she recognized from his dad drinking. But there was something else in there, too.

He nodded. Where was his dad? Why couldn't he pull into the parking lot?

"Like them?" With her free hand—the one not on his boob— she placed a hand on one of hers. Zachariah felt his eyes widen.

His fingers pressed tight against the cool surface of the sauce bottleneck. He felt himself getting hard.

He nodded.

"Why?"

What could he say?

"Gumdrops?"

As she laughed her hand came off Zachariah's boob. "Not candy. My tits."

He had no idea what to say.

"Yes."

"Ever seen any before?"

He couldn't lie. She'd know.

"No."

"Can I have a gumdrop?"

He held the bag out, trembling. She removed the hand from her boob and took it.

"Thanks, Tietz."

She shook the bag over her open mouth. A few of the gumdrops made it inside. Most fell to the ground.

"I don't know if you know this," she said, returning the hand with the bag to her breast, "but my mom is really sick."

He felt himself begin to tremble harder.

"I was wondering if you could help her out."

Zachariah didn't understand. Help her out?

I don't want her to hurt me, he thought.

"What do you mean?"

"She needs money," Dixon Dove said.

She removed the hand and the bag from her boob and shook the remaining gumdrops into the hand that had been on him. She jammed them all in her mouth and chewed thoughtfully.

Zachariah watched her, fascinated. She smiled and returned a hand to her boob.

She put the other hand on him. Down there.

He couldn't look away from her eyes. She smiled and chewed. When her mouth was empty, she said, "You want to help, don't you, Tietz?"

He stuck his free hand into his pants pocket and began fumbling for his change, all the while feeling her hand resting still on his boner.

"Here," he said, finally extracting the bills from his pants.

"Thanks very much," she said, taking the hand from her breast to retrieve the money. "My mom appreciates it."

She stood, still grinning.

He wanted her to stay there. With her hand on him.

He needed to say something to her. So she would stay.

"Where did you get them?"

"Get what, Tietz?"

"Those fireworks."

"Fireworks?"

"At the Pines."

"What do you know about fireworks at the Pines?"

"I saw you there," he said. "The other day."

She took her hand from him. "You were spying on me?"

"No, I just . . ."

"You were spying on me!" She put both hands on his breasts and heaved. He went pinwheeling backward into the wall of the L'il Bee. He felt the barbecue sauce fly up out of his hand. As he gasped for breath the bottle landed with a dull thunk.

Dixon Dove half-dragged, half-pushed him around the corner of the store. She kicked him in the butt. He went sprawling, stomach first, into the dirt.

"You know who spies on people? Pervs spy on people!"

He felt himself trembling anew. Why had he said that? He should've known she'd get mad.

He wished he had done something. Or could do something. Hit her. Kick her. Anything. He knew he wasn't supposed to hit girls. But everyone in school made fun of him already. His life would be better if she wasn't in it. And the other kids might leave him alone, at least for a little while.

His trembling grew stronger.

I just want this to be over.

"Get up, perv," she said, pulling the back of his jeans. He put his hands on the ground, pushup style, and lifted his body. He felt a rock dig into his knee.

"Fucking Tietz," she said, facing him. "Three dollars. Spending all your money on candy."

"I haven't had candy in months," he said.

"You're standing around eating gumdrops. Thanks for those, by the way," she said. "And thanks for the barbecue sauce."

He felt a fresh wave of panic hit and started speaking before he realized he was doing so. Again. "No. You can't. I got that for my dad. He'll be mad if I don't have a bottle."

She grabbed and twisted one of his tietz. He howled and tried to push her away. But her grip was too tight.

Then the other one.

He felt himself losing control.

No, he thought. I can't cry in front of Dixon Dove.

But his breath came in stuttered gasps. He felt tears, thick with face paint, run down his cheeks.

He heard her footsteps walking away as he blubbered, eyes stinging. Maybe she's done, he thought. I hope so. I hope she's done.

Had he just used his power? He thought he had—he remembered thinking he wanted things to be over.

Everything would be okay.

He got up.

He was still hard.

But the footsteps came back toward him.

Everything would not be okay.

There was no okay.

He tried to calm himself, but was crying so hard he could barely see. He felt the ghost imprints of her fingers and nails in his tietz. And the ghost of her hand on his boner.

But that wasn't the worst of it.

He knew he was unable to act.

No matter the brand of humiliation inflicted on him, he could not stand up for himself.

He could not fight back.

He was only able to be acted upon. Not to act.

Always a defenseman, never a striker.

He was powerless.

The interception had been a fluke.

So was his dad, after the game. There was no way he could stop his father.

Or Dixon Dove.

Or the kids at school.

A breaking sound, but controlled. A tearing.

His nostrils filled with sweetness.

He felt a thick liquid sensation atop his head.

"There," she said. "You'll have the bottle for your dad."

22.

His first question: how do you know Sheila?

Couldn't say I don't know her. Which was the truth. So he said the other truth: she's my friend's boss. Artie Travers. Know him?

Ahmed shook his head. I do not. But I know Sheila. I trust her.

Weird. The whole thing. Getting an interview. With this guy.

But he was nice. Smiling. Gave him a bottle of water. Smelled like cologne. Shiny button-up shirt.

Not many people were nice like this. Sheila, Artie, Pattersons. Pretty much it.

So:

Roy, why did you decide to join our military?

Finished high school. No money for college. A chance to see the world. Thought about the GI Bill. Not for me. No good at school. Like cars. Trucks. Working on them. Over there. Want to stick with it. Might like it. Always happy doing it.

Thought about Artie, Sheila. Didn't say might want to work at a real garage later.

A Purple Heart?

Said, wounded. Leg. Got sent back. No permanent damage.

You are very fortunate, my friend.

They all said that. All of them. Sometimes "my brother." But same thing. Always wanted to say you're not my friend. We just met. But never did.

I am.

Be even more fortunate if this job works out. From an Afghani guy. What would Peck think? Probably that it was funny. Sense of humor. Took a crap in a paper bag once. Came back with the mail. Here you go, guys. Passed everything out. Sweeney didn't even notice there was no address. No nothing. Just a paper bag. Opened it. Oh man, someone took a shit in a bag! It's because I give a shit, Peck said. They all laughed. Now you can't say I never gave you shit, because I did. What do you think of that?

Funny. Sweeney. They liked him okay. Didn't know what happened to him. Tour must be over. Never heard back. Tried. Email. PalCorral. Go to the library. Try again.

Ahmed said I am very fortunate too, my friend. I came here on a student visa in the seventies. I completed an MBA at the University of New Hampshire. It took several years to accrue enough capital to begin working for myself.

Impressed by that, accrue. His English was real good.

I saw that automobiles were an excellent opportunity. People will always need them. So I decided that a business that worked to maintain them would be very wise. And good for the community. When people know there is an honest businessman in the community, there is one less thing to worry about. This is why I have decided to open a new franchise in Wilburton. People have come to trust my business. They drive miles to get their oil changed. I will provide the same high level of service there in a more convenient fashion.

Liked talking to him. Wanted to ask questions. About what it was like. Almost asked when the Russia war started, before or after. He knew he should know. Should remember. Couldn't. They talked about it in training. History. Easier to remember it there. Different groups. Factions. Couldn't remember them. Never used them any more. Faded. Like in high school. French. Took it because Auntie Blake told him to. She said it's a better decision than Spanish, Roy. In case you want to go to Canada. No use going to Mexico, with their drug war. French is a much better decision. He got Ds. Hard to speak it. He could understand Ms. LaPierre sometimes. But couldn't remember now.

So I have not been directly involved, Ahmed said. I have watched from afar. I feel strongly for all those involved. It pains me to see such conflict. I am grateful to the United States military for the aid they have provided toward restoring peace to the region. I thank you for your service.

You're welcome.

When might you be able to start?

Right away, he said. Hoped he didn't sound too excited. Wanted to get a job. Felt stupid sitting all the time. The house kept getting colder. Heat. Oil. Six hundred bucks a tank. Called them up. Said can I get fifty gallons? Minimum of a hundred. We have to fill the truck. Get it out there. Smallest order we can do. He didn't have the money. Still waiting for his check. Get the job, fill the tank. Tenants downstairs used theirs. That helped. Floor felt warm under his feet in the morning. But not enough. Wanted them to turn it up. Like ninety.

You will have a two week training period. This will pay minimum wage. Once you have completed training your pay will be twelve dollars an hour. This is our starting rate. From there you will be reviewed every six months. You will have the opportunity to become a supervisor if you are good at the job and a position opens up. There may be more expansion depending on the success of the Wilburton location. We would like to open another branch in Haughton.

Okay, he said.

Good money. Not have to worry. Fill the tank. Get a second beer every time. Listen, Patterson, I have a job now. But she was okay. Hadn't let the kid know he played pool. Liked that. He'd give her a better tip. Buy her a beer.

He could save. Get a new place. A lease. They gave deposits back. Investment in the future. Sounded good. Look around. Get a car. Hopefully work, routine, no headache. Easy. Bike for sure. Go see Artie after work. After they finished their shifts. At their garages. Compare notes. Swap stories. Drink beers. Sounded great.

Ahmed tapped his phone. Nice one. Touch screen. He could get one. Drop the prepaid. Never carried it. No one called. But he could find out about the Sox. Pats. Read the box scores. Not go to the library so much.

Today is Thursday, Ahmed said. You will start Monday. Except it sounded like a question. Monday?

I can do Monday. Thought it sounded good. Important. Like he had other things to set aside.

The Auto Emporium opens at eight, Ahmed said. Please be here at seven thirty. Luis and Mark will show you around.

You will need to bring your documentation for paperwork. W-2. I-9.

Forgot about that stuff. Been a while. Enlistment. Before that the mill. Trays in boxes all day. Took years to get promoted. Bags.

But the other mills closed. Seniority. Got bumped. Couldn't find anything. Over and over. Before, since. Applications.

Have to find his birth certificate. Blank next to father. Social security card. Military ID. Not sure what else.

Ahmed stood. Stuck his hand out. The cologne smell again, stronger. Thank you, Roy, he said. I'm sure you will be a great employee.

He stood. I'm sure I will be, too. Thank you, Ahmed.

He looked around the office. Clean. But not tidy. Piled papers. Nice enough. Felt himself smiling.

Walked out to the lobby. Big TV, magazines.

He'd get a drink. To celebrate. Except no place in town was open. Patterson's wouldn't be until later. The Bellweather closed while he was overseas. Sad about that. Never got to go. Remembered he could smell it when he walked by on the way to the mill job. Old beers and hamburger patties. Urinal pucks. Thought he'd go when he turned twenty-one. But he never did. Stabbing. Drug deal. Oxy. Boards over the windows.

He walked downtown. Asian place. Didn't like it. And food at home. Rice. Beans. Ramen.

But the Pattersons' other place. Ice cream. Couldn't remember the last time he had any. Liked it. Never bought it. Too expensive.

Checked his wallet. Six bucks. Enough for a few beers. Or a cone. Check coming soon. Had a job. Could play some pool. Make some money. Deserved it. Finally had a job.

The Double Scoop.

Went in. Recognized him right away, writing in a notebook. The fat kid. No paint. But still.

Patterson behind the counter. Smiled. Hello, Roy, she said. I don't think I've ever seen you in here before.

Never been, Roy said. First time.

Thanks for coming! What would you like?

I don't know.

Chocolate or vanilla?

Had those before. And strawberry. Didn't want those. Something new. Like a beer during the day. To celebrate.

I just got a job, he said.

No kidding! Where?

Auto Emporium.

Ahmed, Patterson said. He's a good guy. Comes in a lot. He brings his kids.

He has kids?

Yes, she said.

It surprised him. Didn't know why. Plenty of them did. Overseas they were everywhere. Peck. Why would these fucking people bring more mouths into this miserable world? Not enough food to go around. Fucking animals. Never heard of a condom before. Or pulling out. It's not Allah's way or some shit. Or maybe they're just stupid.

What does he get?

Something different every time.

He looked at the flavors on the chalkboard. Rum raisin. Butter crunch. Berry blast.

Pick out something new for me, he said. Something I've never had.

23.

THAT GUY GARY IS NO BIG deal.

He was looking at my ass and tits especially the whole shift, but except for this one time his hand kinda brushed my ass when he was walking by, it was fine.

Besides, he had me on register. The last thing. I think I'm gonna get stuck there a lot because I'm fast. That's what he told me at the end of the shift when he had me come into his office. Dalton heard him ask me to come in and rolled his eyes.

People are weird. Like they haven't been to Burger Hut a million times. They stand there and try to figure out what to order even though they've been there for five minutes looking at the menu the whole time. I'm waiting at the register with all these buzzers going off in the back while they stand there. A couple of times I started over toward the fry machine without thinking about it and was like hah, whoops, I'm on register. Then another buzzer would go off while the same person stood there, still trying to decide.

It was like that all day. And questions.

That's how it happened. I was on register and this lady came up and said what are your healthy dietary alternatives? I wanted to be like lady, you're in Burger Hut, there are no healthy alternatives, so just get a Downtown Deluxe. But instead I was like the Salad Supremo is very healthy. She said I was thinking more burger than salad. I said I wasn't sure. And Gary walked by. He said something about the Lean Supreme being the most health-conscious choice, and would she like to try one on the house? She said that would be delightful. Just like that: that would be delightful.

So when I finished the shift, Gary asked me into his office and Dalton was like good luck. I went in. It's this tiny little room the size of a closet in the back and has all these black and white TVs that show everyone working. He can sit there and watch everyone make burgers.

He said Dixon, we have not had the pleasure of working together since you started here.

I said no.

Then he goes this is the last of your training shifts, right?

I said right. Then he went on about how Burger Hut prides itself on offering a variety of healthy, nutritious food. He pointed to the TVs. In addition to using these monitors I occasionally listen in on transactions to make sure they are satisfactory. I have been paying special attention to yours today, since we have never worked together and since you are at the end of your training. What I have seen has largely been outstanding. I was particularly impressed with your speed on the register. You don't make many mistakes.

He was looking at me like he wanted me to say something. I didn't really know what, so I nodded and said thanks.

Then he said it's obvious to me you're good with your hands.

He waited again and I said thanks again.

After a second he said here, let me show you something.

He put one hand under his desk. Then a second later I could hear the restaurant.

Jack was on register: Welcome to Burger Hut. May I take your order?

A skinny girl with a kid was on one of the TVs looking up at the menu. She said uh. Then I'd like a Downtown Deluxe combo and a kid's meal.

He said I watched you today. I was also listening to you. You did a good job. You're very good with customers. For the most part. But there was one transaction that worried me.

Jack's voice cut out halfway through. That'll be nine dol—

I said you mean what I said about the healthy choices?

Gary said while you may have a way with customers, there's more to it than your natural talent. I came out of the back room because I recognized the customer. She can be difficult with her questions.

I nodded.

At the beginning of your training you were provided with menu descriptions for the items we serve, complete with nutritional information.

I hadn't looked at it since.

Before you appear on the floor, you need to know all the information contained in that packet. The healthy alternatives are there. If a customer asks—and they will—you need to know which items contain the fewest calories and the least fat and so on.

I told him I said salad.

He said salad is a good choice. But not everyone comes to Burger Hut for salad. Burger is in the name. They come for them.

I said okay.

He said I understand you're almost done with your training, but without the kind of knowledge we're looking for I'm afraid you might not be ready to start on the floor.

I don't want any more training shifts. Two-fifty an hour, or whatever it is. I want to get paid.

Without really thinking about it I pulled my shirt up and showed him my bra.

You wanna see these?

He started smiling real big. He said yes, I do.

I'll be ready to start working, right?

He said I can trust you to study the menu descriptions on your own.

I held up my shirt with my chin and pushed my bra down so he could see my tits. I gave them a shake and stood there for a sec before I pulled my bra back up and let my shirt down.

He said I'm glad we have this understanding. You'll be on the schedule.

* * *

I'D GONE BY BEFORE WORK AND there weren't any unlocked so I had to hitch. I didn't think about what would happen on a weekend, when there was no one there.

Pretty much right away some old guy with a pickup pulled over and asked me where I was going. I told him Burger Hut and he said get in the back. It was cold. I wanted to be in the cab with him. I had my knife with me.

I decided to just walk home instead of hitching but this car pulled up. It was Ding.

You need a ride someplace?

I said L'il Bee.

He said one ride to L'il Bee, coming right up.

I got in and showed him my tits right away. Twice in the same day. I never did that before.

He said very nice and passed me a flask. Whiskey. I took a pull.

Then he said we haven't been seeing as much of each other as we used to.

I said yeah, I know. I've been working.

Don't you like fireworks any more?

I said they're cool, but I'm trying to save. I told you that.

He asked where I was gonna move. I told him I wasn't sure yet. Just out.

He said you can always come to my place. I have a couch. My rates are very affordable.

I said thanks. I'll think about it.

Then he goes you know, if you're looking to make some real money there are better ways to do it than Burger Hut. You work there what, forty hours a week?

I said twenty. Part time.

He said why only twenty? I said school.

You do any good? In school?

I said you know.

He said if you have a job, why don't you work full-time? Make more loot. Drop out.

I said my mom's boyfriend would beat the shit out of me if I did.

He said well, maybe you need to start your own business, like me.

I said yeah, maybe.

Then he goes you can set up your own hours and starts laughing. Work from home. Think about it. I can set you up. You probably know a lot more kids than I do. Uh, kids your age, I mean. Be a chip off the old block. Just like your brother.

I was like wait, what?

He goes come on. You must know he deals.

I was like bullshit.

But then I thought about it. He doesn't work. And he smokes tons of weed. Tons.

I thought he bought from Steve. But I didn't think about where he got the money.

What was all this shit about me pinching off his stash the other day? If he deals?

I wanted to ask Ding more questions but we pulled into the parking lot.

Here you go. Think about what I said. Open your own franchise.

I was like thanks and got out.

* * *

I still don't know how I'm gonna get to work. I don't have a bike. I guess I can buy one.

* * *

I took some money out of my stash and went down to the sporting goods store today before work. I bought a bike and a lock. I was the only person in there. It was pretty much the cheapest girl bike they had. And the lock I got is really thick. The guy tried to sell me a helmet but I don't want to look like a tool bag biking around.

I'm out two hundred bucks.

I don't usually go to that plaza. It's also got a drugstore and a liquor store. There's good shit there. I'll have to remember it. Not as many wallets, but I got a laptop! So the bike will be discount when I sell it to Ding.

I guess maybe I thought Ross was doing the same thing.

* * *

Work today was okay. It didn't feel different. I clocked in and got on sandwich with Dalton.

He was like what happened yesterday? I told him I passed my menu test. He said I didn't have to take one. I was like I don't know.

Then he said that lady's rough. From yesterday. If I was up there I would have told you but I was on grill. I said you know her? He was like yeah, Barbara. She knows the answers to all the questions but asks anyway. I said why? and he said to get free food when you fuck up. He said was that it?

I was like what do you mean? and he said, well, you know that guy's got a rep, right? I was like yeah. He said I saw him touch your ass yesterday.

I was like that was an accident.

He was like come on girl, are you dumb?

I said I don't think it'll happen again. It's fine.

I didn't think of it until today. Until then. Maybe him not touching my ass is gonna make people notice. I mean, Dalton saw him do it yesterday, so if he stops people will think something is wrong. Maybe I should tell Gary to grab it and I'll tell him to stop. But if I do that he'll get mad.

I don't know.

Maybe I should quit, like everyone says. Deal. Like Ross.

I can't believe I didn't figure it out. But it makes sense. He's always at school. I thought it was for practice. Or lifting weights.

Anyway, I did early shift, so it was Judy all day. She came by and congratulated me and said we need to talk in the office.

She asked if I had ever been in there before. I said yeah, when I was talking to Gary.

She said this is about him. He can be out of line. I was like what do you mean? and she said to women. The only way to deal with him is to set boundaries. I was like what do you mean again and she said the first time he lays a finger on you tell him to keep his hands to himself. He's all bark, you understand?

I said yeah.

She said girls who do not put their foot down quit. And you seem like the kind of girl I wouldn't mind working with. I don't say that to everyone. So be careful.

I said thanks.

24.

ZACHARIAH LOVED MAKING BREAD. THE FIRST time, years ago in home ec, his teacher (what was her name? he couldn't remember) showed him the process. His bread came out perfectly. He never needed a recipe again after that. And not just bread—everything he baked or cooked was great.

He mixed the ingredients gently. One-handed wasn't so hard. He just needed to slow the process was all. But the pain was all over. Back, chest. Muscles he didn't know he had screamed in protest as he moved. And the blood in his pee, though starting to subside, was still more concentrated than he'd ever seen it.

The pain was a constant reminder of how stupid he'd been in thinking he had powers. Or could control footballs with his mind. Or people.

But the prospect of Zachariah's life staying as it had been, staying in Armbrister, was too much to bear—worse than a dozen of his dad's beatings. There had to be something else besides getting picked on every day, then when he finished school, going to work at the mill. He had to finish *Love Balloon*. And even that might not work. He had to think it would, but he knew it probably wouldn't.

If he'd had powers, he could have used them the day before to keep himself from getting picked on.

Every day he removed his jacket when he arrived at school. The day before he'd done so immediately upon entering the building, walking right past Dixon Dove's locker in the process. She wasn't there, thank God. Neither, he noticed, was the old, smiling security guard.

Had he kept his jacket on, maybe it would have been okay. But he hadn't thought it through.

Zachariah realized he did that sometimes. Like at the L'il Bee. The guy behind the counter might have helped if he'd run in and said listen, I just got in a fight and my dad will kill me if I don't have a bottle of barbecue sauce when he gets back from the liquor store. The first one, dripping thickly from his head, would have been all the proof he needed. Please, Zachariah could have said. I'll pay you back.

But he hadn't run in. He'd frozen when Dixon Dove came around the corner. And she'd left, laughing, after upending the bottle over his head. He'd sat against the back wall, unable to stop his sobbing.

The realization that he'd been lying to himself hurt more than the fresh finger marks in his tietz, or the mix of sauce and paint in his eyes. He'd pretended that his weight gain had been balanced by getting a superpower, like in the movies. Which couldn't happen. He wanted it to and had tried to convince himself, time and again, that it had. Even though he forgot for days at a time, while working on *Love Balloon* or making bread, that he—supposedly—had powers. And even though he still got picked on all the time. And even though his dad hit him.

But the jacket came off and everyone was on him. He'd wear it from now on, but word would get around, if it hadn't already. It always did.

He had to find some way to keep Dixon Dove at bay. He couldn't fight her—maybe he could have before, had he not frozen, but certainly not now, with his cast. And hoping his arm would cause her to leave him alone was stupid. He couldn't sit around and hope. Not anymore.

He had to do something.

He greased the pan and put his dough on the metal table, dusted with flour. Kneading took more time one-handed.

The way she had touched him. Before she got mad at him— before she called him a perv—he felt like he was talking to her. Like they could be friends. If there was some way to impress her, maybe she'd do it again.

And as he mixed he had an idea.

* * *

The librarians were nicer to him than usual.

"Oh," Ms. Petrie said, "what happened?"

He thought back to what his dad said in the car.

"I fell down the basement stairs," he said.

She looked at him hard. "Really?"

He nodded. "I slipped. On the rug in front of them."

She kept her hard look.

"I was getting some meat. Out of the freezer."

Her face softened. "Well, I'm sorry to hear it."

There was nothing in the basement except boxes of his mother's old stuff his dad didn't ever throw away. If anyone came, they'd see this. And through the story.

He didn't want to go to a boy's home. Even though, in the back of his mind, he thought it might not be so bad. The kids there wouldn't know about him pissing his pants. Or that he'd been a normal kid at the end of last year.

But it would be bad. He knew it.

Why did he always do that? Lie to himself? Try to convince himself about things that weren't real?

He had to stop.

25.

Stepped outside. Couldn't tell how cold until then. Whatever weather was in the apartment stayed there. Sweater, sweatshirt. Bedroom freezing. Window frame. Air coming in. Stuffed it. Old socks. Helped a little. Bought the plastic. Put it over the glass. No hair dryer. Couldn't afford one. Thought the plastic helped. Maybe only wanted it to.

Warmer outside than in. On his walk to work. Liked to think that. "I'm going to work." Even though it was training. He followed the guy. Mark. Always smoking. Radio on a news station. That's what Doris likes, Mark said. Keeps her informed. He liked music better. But easier with news. Didn't have to worry. No headaches.

After work Mark brought out beers. Said here, man. Have one. Kept him on for close. Said eight to five was opening. But you should see everything. Meant see after we're done. Understood that. Everyone sat. Watched the Celtics game on TV. Drank beers. Talked about cars. Customers. No one paid attention to him but Mark.

Wasn't hard. Tricky maybe. Hard to figure out the lifts. The nozzles. But not bad. Little things in each one. Drains. Filter sizes. Where fluids were. Which kind. A lot to remember. Charts helped. But he wanted to know. You have to do everything once to get it, Mark said. Second day. Maybe more than once. But you'll get it. He smoked and asked war questions. Didn't mind, mostly. Nice to be asked. Talk to someone.

Did you kill guys?

No one ever asked that. Who would? Artie, maybe. But he didn't. Let him talk when he wanted to.

Yeah.

A lot?

Well, he said.

They had been driving to the village. Him in the back. Bunch of guys. No canopy. Usually played music. Psych them out. None that time. Remembered that. Didn't know why. They usually did.

Saw three. Behind a dune. One had a grenade. Cocked back to throw. Shot him first. Without even thinking. Like he wasn't in his head. No thoughts. Just shooting. Watched himself do it. From above. Rifle on his back then in his hand and opened up and the grenade the guy was cocking stayed back there and after he shot and shot it exploded.

The other two had rifles. Them next. First went down hard. Both got off shots. One missed his face. Felt the air change. Like a pull. Heard bullets hit. Behind. A clang. Thump. Scream. Didn't know who. A clang. Clangclang. Back there with Long, Donaldson, a few others.

The other one kept shooting. Got him. Headshot. Red spray, gray. Hung there for a second in a cloud. Too far away to taste it. Like metal in his mouth. But that was later. Body fell backward shooting into the air. Like a sack of potatoes. Screams. I'm hit oh fuck I'm hit aaaaaaaagggghh. Hit the deck. Waited for more.

None came.

Truck stopped. Long back there. Working on Donaldson. That's who it was. Leg. Thigh. Didn't look bad. Not much blood. Wouldn't know it by the screaming. Aggggghhhh it fucking hurts. Long saying it's not bad, man, Jesus shut up already. Arrrrghhhhh hurry up, man, gahhhhhhgh.

Peck in the passenger seat. Rifle out his window. Jumped out. Walked around the back. Crouched. Hand on his Cowboys star. That was some shooting, Eggleton.

He watched himself say, that guy had a grenade. He was trying to kill us.

Their rifles woulda finished the rest of us, Long said. He was holding Donaldson's leg. You saved our asses.

Didn't think. Saw them, reacted. Just like he was trained. Protect your buddies. Your brothers.

Someone should put you up for a star, Frick said.

Face flushed. Felt it. A star. Get home. Show Auntie Blake. Look at this. War hero. Saved some guys. But she died. Never got to tell her. And they never recommended him. Or they did and nothing happened. Maybe because of the prisoners, and what happened with Peck, Long. Could you take back paperwork? Lose it?

He didn't tell Mark about going back out because of Donaldson. To get revenge. Any of the other stuff. The video. Could've. Would've been easy. AC/DC blasting. On the drive, in the room. The video. Everybody ready. Looking. For someone. Knew he shouldn't. But wanted to.

Wow, man. That's fucked up.

Yeah. Felt the bullets go by. Inches.

Seriously.

After, with beers, Mark told Luis that Roy killed three dudes over there.

No shit, Luis said. They shootin' at you?

Yeah. Me and my buddies.

How did it feel?

Didn't feel like anything. Didn't feel bad. If he hadn't shot, more guys might've died. Him. He might have died. Or the grenade might have hit him. Lose an arm, leg. Wheelchair. Auntie Blake pushing him around. Mad at him for getting hit. Sighing all the time. Reminding him. But she died. While he was over there. Wasn't immediate family. Could've fought for time off to go to her funeral. Didn't want to. Didn't feel that bad.

The next day felt different. Everyone. Got quiet. Then started talking again. Hey, man, what's up? Like the teacher walked into the room. Except they talked to him. Maybe like Peck. Respect. Because he killed. Mark the same, though. Just everyone else. Who hadn't really talked to him. All introduced themselves. Marco. Juan. Dmitry. Andy. Asked how he was doing. If he needed help. That night, close again. Beers. SportsCenter. Then to Patterson's. Didn't ask if they wanted to come. Should've. They would. More beers. Pool. Lefty. Against no one. Wasn't that good. Too much to drink. Empty stomach. Still did that sometimes. Three he felt. Wasn't bad if he ate. Mac and cheese, ramen cups. But he didn't. Couldn't sink his shots. Warm, though. Garage was, too. But drafty. Moved around a lot. Helped.

No hurry to go home. Maybe work as much as he could. Overtime. Senior guys would get hours. He'd do it for free. Liked them. Sitting and bullshitting after work. Even during. Got their stories.

At home, letter on the table. Cessation of benefits. Good timing. Right when he got a job. He'd have to call the office. Hated that. Waiting on the phone. Dealing with robots. Especially after working. Talking all day. To people.

They talked about Ahmed. Never like oh, he's from overseas. Wasn't that. Everyone liked him. Dmitry was going to manage the new place. Mark was taking Dmitry's job as Armbrister manager. He said Ahmed pays more than anyone. Everyone stays because he treats us good. Health insurance. Can you believe that shit? And dental! Fuckin' A. I hadn't been to the dentist in ten years before I started.

Had been in the garage so much. Since Monday. No walks. Missed them. But standing all day felt good. Leg felt strong. And not sitting. Bad for you. Walk on weekends. Days off. Weird fall. Cold but not too cold. Apartment made it feel colder. But sidewalk icy on the way down. Walked slow. Didn't mind. Walk warmed him up. Then the garage would. It'd be a while. Doris said because of his hire date the first check would be three weeks. He could do it. But it'd be tight. Running out of money. Oil could wait. Cold at night, but close the place whether he got paid or not, then Patterson's and to bed early. Stay warm like that. Get oil with second check. Hopefully wouldn't need it much. Doubted that. Garage news stories said coldest in twenty years. Colder in his apartment. Maybe the library on days off. Stay warm that way. Buy himself real cheese instead of that powdered shit. Maybe a steak. Figure out how to cook it in a pan. Like Auntie Blake. When he graduated. I do not agree with your choices, Royal, but I respect them. I can respect your decision. He thought about that. Thought it meant she was happy he left. That he was paying his own way. Even though he gave her rent money before he lost the mill job. Didn't save anything. Stupid.

Should have. Could have bought some oil. But he went out with Artie. Sox games. Loading dock beers. Great times. Wouldn't trade them. But money would buy heat.

Mark there smoking already. Two packs a day, he said. How much did Artie smoke? He'd ask. Hadn't talked to Artie since he started. They'd go out. Get beers. Compare notes. After the oil maybe a car. Thought it would be okay. Could drive to see Artie. No music. Just news. Wouldn't have to walk. Too cold. Didn't think Christa would mind. She was okay.

Hey, man, good morning.

Good morning.

What's new?

Not much, he said. Wanted to tell him about the letter the same way he wanted to tell him about the prisoner. Didn't. Knew he shouldn't. Wanted to. Probably okay. But too soon. Went over to Patterson's. Came home. Went to bed.

You go there a lot?

Yeah, he said. I play pool.

Any good?

He shrugged. I'm okay.

I never got any good at pool. Just drinking.

Roy laughed. You should come sometime.

Maybe I will.

Hang out after work watching the Celtics, then go play pool. Sounded good. Maybe Artie could go. Hey. This is my friend Mark. Manages Auto Emporium. They could go see the Sox. Hang out on weekends. Maybe go camping. Might show Mark his game. Watch this, he'd say. Start playing lefty. Guys would come in. Take them on. Lose the first few. Then switch. Win big. Make money. Beers all night.

Ahmed usually comes in on Thursdays, Mark said. Just so you know. You're doing good.

What's it like?

Just keep doing what you're doing.

What's that?

Ask questions. Pay attention. You'll be fine.

Okay. Anything else today?

Same as usual.

26.

When I got up for school Don was on the couch. I thought he was passed out but when I walked by he said goin' to work? I said no, school.

Then he was like you're gonna mish me when I'm gone.

He was drunk at seven in the morning.

I asked when he was leaving, and he said in a few weeks. Then he said I'm gonna shpend my time on thish couch. And burped. It was a good one.

I told him I had to go to school. He said where'd you get that bike in the backyard? I said that's my bike. He asked where I got the money to buy it and I told him at work. He said Gary Stites—which he slurred, Shtaytz—said you just finished training.

I forgot Don knew him so I said yeah, I borrowed some money from a guy at work. He said it better not be shtolen and I said no, it's not, I told you I bought it. And he said it better not be dirty. I was like what do you mean? and he said you're making minimum wage over there so how can you find someone to borrow money from? Something shtinks.

I said Don, I have to go to school and he was like if the bike isn't shtolen the money's from shomeplace elshe. I said I told you,

I'm borrowing it from a guy at work and he said bullshit. Except he yelled it.

He almost fell when he stood up. He said I don't think it's drugsh. You don't sheem the type. I don't know what he meant by that. Then he goes it's boysh, ishn't it? I was like no, it's from a guy at work and he was like it's boysh. I wanted to be like Don, like this girl Mary but I thought that would piss him off. He said you're turning into a slut. I knew it. You'll get knocked up. Your poor mother's heart is going to break when I tell her. I was like no, I borrowed the money.

I remembered the laptop in my room. And the money. He probably goes in there and snoops when I'm at school. The fireworks. This. Jesus, all the stuff on here. I said I forgot a book, Don, I'll be right back. He started yelling again. He was like bullshit, get back here. I went to my room and as fast as I could got everything from their hiding places into my bag. Then I took *Catch-22* out and when I went back I was carrying it.

I was like Don, I'm late. He yelled since when do you give a fuck about school? I said I wanted to make something of myself and he said yeah, a whore and started toward me. He was standing in the way of both doors. I was like come on, Don, I'm late and he said where did you get the money? I said I told you, I borrowed it and he said I don't believe you, you're turning into a floozy. I laughed because come on, floozy? I couldn't help it. He said what the fuck are you laughing at? and I said floozy. No one talks like that. He said a fucking whore, then, and was like you're lying about shome-thing. Either that bike is shtolen or the money is. I said let me out.

He wouldn't.

I can't believe he fell for this shit. I looked at the door and was all Mom, what are you doing back so early? He was like wha—?

and turned to look at the door, which of course was still closed. When he did that I pushed his gut with both hands and my book and his arms started spinning. He fell back against the lamp and was all whoomph when he hit. I got out of there and around back to my bike. Of course it was locked and at first I thought I left the key inside and I'd have to go back in to get it but I had it in my pocket. It took a few seconds to undo it because my hands were shaking. He came to the front door just as I was leaving, yelling come back, you little shlut.

I had to stop I was shaking so bad. I still am. I'm behind the L'il Bee.

I didn't even think of Don and the bike.

* * *

At school today everyone kinda stopped talking when they saw me, then they'd start up again when I went by. I could feel their eyes.

I thought it was about work. Somehow someone found out about me showing my tits to Gary.

I looked around for Mary. But I saw Dalton first.

He said are you okay?

I was like what are you talking about?

He said you don't know?

I was like know what?

He said it's about your brother.

I was like my brother? And he said yeah. The football team got drug tested.

I said why? and he said random. Their number came up. I was like oh, no and he said yeah, your brother and four other players failed. I asked what was gonna happen. He said he didn't know. Maybe Ross would be suspended. He probably won't be in the playoffs.

Dalton said I have to go to class. He asked if he'd see me at work and I said yeah even though I couldn't remember my schedule.

I went to history and could hear everyone's conversations about the team like I wasn't even there.

The recruiters will hear about this. It'll be in the papers and on the Internet. Then they won't touch him.

Don is gonna be PISSED.

At lunch I went to the football table and asked if any of them had seen my brother. I said his name and they all looked at me like they didn't hear me. Then one guy said he left when he heard.

I couldn't do school. Not with everyone looking at me like that. And Don was gonna be wasted on the couch. So I got my bike off the rack and went over to the L'il Bee and went up the path as far as I could. I didn't even make it to the hearse.

I locked the back tire to the frame and stashed it behind some trees. Then I walked the rest of the way. No one was at the quarry. I half-expected to see Steve, or Earl.

Then I smelled weed.

I followed the path like I was going out to the Pines. The smell was coming from somewhere to the left. All the little branches and trees were bent.

I tried to get in and someone yelled who's there? I was like it's your sister, dumb-ass. I walked all the way in and there he was, sitting on the ground crossed-legged, smoking a big one.

He said what are you doing here? as he put it out on his palm.

I said everyone at school was looking at me.

He said you're telling me.

I was like when did you take the test?

He said months ago. They gave us a day's notice. I drank as much water as I could the day before and took some pills to help flush my system. But it didn't work. I thought maybe it did because they never said anything. Guess not.

I was like whoa.

He said yeah. Then he said all the recruiters are gonna hear about this. I probably won't get into Nebraska. Or anywhere else.

I was like someone will take you. He said I don't know. I never heard of schools taking guys who've failed a weed test.

I said I wasn't sure you wanted to go.

He said I guess I thought I didn't want to, but now that maybe I can't I want to. Does that make sense?

I said yeah.

He said even though I wasn't sure if I liked football, now that I might not be able to go I know I like Armbrister even less.

I was like no shit.

He said hopefully some school will take me so I can get out of here. No matter how shitty it is. Even if it's like the Tech in Concord or something, I won't have to be in this stupid town anymore. Everyone always looking at me like they know me.

I said Concord's okay. Manchester.

He was like Manch Vegas? No way.

I said it must be nice to have a choice.

He was like you always do. But I might have fucked mine up. Then he was like what's yours?

What?

Your choice.

I said I don't know.

Then I told him I wanna save money and move.

He took out a lighter and asked if I wanted to hit it. I said sure. He relit the joint and passed it to me. I took a big haul. Look, I said, I'm gonna go.

He said don't tell Mom you saw me. Or Don.

I told him I wouldn't.

* * *

I biked around for a while. Then I went home.

There was some guy by the front door. He was skinny and bald, with big glasses. I could beat him up one-handed. He was a reporter, asked me if I had any comment on the suspension of Ross Dove for the rest of the football season. I said no and went around the back.

No Mom. I guess she's at work. And no Don. Thank God. I thought he'd have his fat ass on the couch. But where else was I supposed to go?

I wish I could see Mary.

I guess I'm still a little high. There's still that guy outside. Maybe he's waiting for Ross. Or Mom. Or Don. Anyone.

27.

WELCOME BACK TO *LOVE BALLOON*, ZACK FOX says.

The cameras cut to the contestants—nine, now—standing on risers on the dark soundstage. Behind them Jenna's face is on the big screen.

"What's my favorite type of cake?"

"Chocolate," the contestants say in unison. They grin at each other.

"That's right," she says. "I've been having a stressful day at work. I'd like to celebrate the weekend by having some chocolate cake. And you're going to make one for me. You will be given fifty dollars. You'll go to the store and buy all the supplies you'll need. I will judge the two best cakes. I bet you're wondering how I'll know which two cakes are the best."

Everyone nods.

"One of my friends is going to help me out."

Zack Fox smiles. He says, "I'd like to introduce you to celebrity chef Pierre Lefevre!"

Cut to a contestant: "Pierre Lefevre! He's only one of the most famous chefs in the world. He's got restaurants in Paris, Vegas, and New York. And his TV shows are great, too."

Another contestant: "I watch *CookRight with Pierre*. Like, all the time."

And another: "*ChefWars* is my favorite show. I can't believe he's here."

" 'Allo!" he says to the contestants. His catchphrase.

They shout back, " 'ALLO!"

"Today you are going to make a cake for Jenna. I will taste the cakes and decide the winner. The best cake will win three hundred points. And for both finalists, a prize.

On screen, Jenna's face is replaced by a cooking set.

"Pierre Lefevre cookware for you," he says. "The best in the world."

"Now, are you ready?"

"YEAH!"

"To the store."

They pile into SUVs and are driven to FreshMart.

One contestant, a striker, says to the camera, "Cook? I never cooked before. That's why I need to win this thing. So I can get Jenna to cook me whatever I want."

A normal guy says, "My mom and I used to cook all the time. She showed me some tricks."

Another normal guy says, "She said chocolate was her favorite, and I looked it up just in case. I wanted to know how to make good chocolate desserts. And now we have to make one!"

The contestants run around the store. Most congregate in the cake aisle, where they look at boxes of mix. One normal contestant heads straight for the candy aisle.

"Fifty dollars is a lot of money for a cake," he says. "I'd better make it good."

He selects several expensive-looking triangular chocolate bars, then heads for the dairy aisle. Some contestants are already there looking at eggs. He finds heavy cream.

Several aisles away, a striker stands looking at a tub of frosting.

Pierre Lefevre waits by the cash registers. He yells, "FIVE MINUTES!"

Most everyone gets change back when they pay for their groceries.

The SUVs drive the contestants to a new location.

The group is brought inside a huge, plain building, each carrying a bag into an expanse of glistening steel ranges and ovens. Each of nine stations is stocked with cookware: bowls, cake pans, whisks, and spoons.

"You have one hour to make your cake," Pierre Lefevre says. "Begin!"

Some contestants lay their cookware out first, some read cake mix boxes, others immediately dump ingredients into bowls.

"An hour's a long time," one contestant says. "I'll take my time and make sure I do the best job I can."

"I've made cake before," another says. "It's hard to get frosting to look good on a hot cake."

Cut to Pierre Lefevre: "I enjoy watching groups of people cook in my kitchen. Some of them have cooking experience, others do not. It always interests me to see the different approaches people take. But I do not watch too hard because I know I will have to eat from all their cakes. It is hard not to correct them when they make mistakes."

Mix prepared, one contestant pours batter into a rectangular pan. The next adds brown sugar. Another forgets to grease the sides of a round pan. Yet another adds an entire small bottle of vanilla extract. Still another puts a cake into the oven, then turns it on.

The first contestant to get his cake into the oven—who said his mom taught him tricks—removes his cake. He flips the pan upside down and taps gently on the underside. His cake falls onto a serving plate.

"When I saw the cake," he says, "I wasn't that worried. It looked fine. Not perfect, but fine. Plenty of time."

"Ten minutes," Pierre Lefevre says, pacing the kitchen. "Make them look pretty."

"I never made a cake before," one contestant says. "How was I supposed to know you have to grease the pan?"

The contestants are either frosting their cakes or staring into ovens. The first contestant heats a pan of cream on the stove. He pours the hot cream into his bowl of chocolate triangles.

"It looks really bad at first," he says. "It always does. I remember my mom saying that you'll think you made a big mistake. But whisk it, then taste it. You'll be surprised."

He sticks a finger into the mix, then takes a taste and smiles, nodding.

The camera cuts to a digital clock counting down to zero. "FIVE SECONDS," Pierre Lefevre shouts. "THREE."

The contestants put the finishing touches on their cakes.

"Time is up," he says.

The kitchen is instantly clean of all cooking supplies as Pierre stands next to Zack Fox, looking at the line of contestants. On the counter in front of each is either a cake or a pile of scraps.

One says on camera: "I never baked a cake before. Or frosted one."

Another, a striker: "I made layers. I divided the mix into three small pans and joined them with frosting."

Pierre says, "Let's see what we have here, eh?"

"This one," Pierre says after expertly cutting a slice, "is very good, but your frosting is horrible."

"This one is tasteless," Pierre says of another. "Overdone."

Then: "This one is very nice. A little plain in presentation, but nice."

"A little plain," the contestant says, "but nice. Just like me!"

Pierre eats from every cake. The contestant who made layers is singled out—not the most elegant, the chef says, but ambitious—as is the contestant who made his own chocolate sauce.

The plain cake and the chocolate sauce cake are the final two.

The contestant who made the layers says, "Today wasn't my day. I thought the design would be enough. I should have spent more time putting the frosting on. Or let the cake cool a little. I bet that would have helped."

"These two are the best," Pierre Lefevre says. "Congratulations. Both of you win a set of my cookware, plus my new cookbook, *Pierre's Way Every Day*."

The contestants smile and nod.

"If I win *Love Balloon*," one contestant says, "I can cook for Jenna with my new pots and pans."

"I bet you're wondering how I will determine which cake is the victor today," he says.

They both nod.

"The answer is I will not. Jenna will do that for me."

She walks in and stands next to Pierre. The contestants have only ever seen her on-screen.

One contestant, a striker says, "Dude, she's hot. I knew she was a looker because of the TV and all, but man!"

Another: "Whoa!"

Another: "She isn't as tall as I thought."

"Hello, everyone," she says.

Cut to a contestant: "Her voice sounds nicer in person."

"I'm going to sample these two cakes. The best one wins three hundred points. Plus, I'll take the rest home and finish it later."

Everyone laughs.

Cut to a striker: "She can take me home and finish me later."

"Let me try this one first," she says, cutting into the plain cake.

"Wow! This is really good. I didn't think it was going to be anything special—is that a horrible thing to say? It looks so normal. But it's great."

Cut to the contestant who made the cake: "Yeah. Just like me!"

She tries the second cake. "Oh, wow," she says. This cake is good, but the frosting, especially. This isn't store-bought. Someone made this. And it's really good!"

A shot of the second contestant. "Thanks, Mom," he says, "for teaching me how to make chocolate sauce."

"Wow. This is a hard decision."

"Take your time," Zack Fox says.

"It is hard," Pierre Lefevre says. "Both cakes are very good."

"They are," she says. "But you know, after thinking about it, I know which one is the best. It's going to be . . ."

Cut to commercial.

When the show starts again:

"But you know, after thinking about it, I know which one is the best. It's going to be . . . this one."

She points to the plain cake.

"Even though it's not very exciting, and the other one has frosting, I like this one better."

The contestant whoops for joy.

"Excellent choice," Pierre Lefevre says.

Zack Fox, smiling, awards three hundred points.

* * *

Zachariah read back what he wrote.

This is dumb, he thought. It wouldn't happen like this.

For one thing, the plain cake wouldn't even get to the final round. Maybe it tastes good, but the guy who made layers would get further along. Presentation.

Even if he was a striker.

And another thing: she wouldn't pick a cake that tasted worse than the one made with real chocolate. Zachariah couldn't wait for the day when he could afford to make chocolate sauce himself. Whenever it was a birthday—his or his dad's—frosting was always premade, from the store. He couldn't get his dad to buy chocolate bars and cream. Especially now. His dad had been so mad at him, first about the barbecue sauce, then about the cost of his broken arm.

He couldn't keep writing the game show, trying to let losers like himself win. It was broken and he knew it.

He had to do something. He couldn't just wish, or pretend he had powers. Not any more. Not since Dixon Dove.

Instead of writing his game show, he had to work on his plan. Getting everything together. He knew how to impress her.

28.

Shivering in the apartment. Library closed. Too early for pool.

Needed money. Bad. Didn't think the check would come from Ahmed. Worked four days. Training wages. Minimum. But they'd keep it. At least. Might take more. Sue. Hoped not. No way to pay.

Everything going so good. Stupid. Thinking he and Mark were friends. And Artie. Going to see the Sox together. Playing pool. Bars. Hanging out. Now he could never call. Not after Ahmed. Yelled. Maybe cost Mark his promotion. How could you let a trainee do this? A man on the fourth day of the job putting a car on a lift unattended.

Hummer pulled in. Mark said hey, man, check it out. Ever drive one of these over there? Meant Humvee. Knew what he was talking about. Said no, he never drove a Hummer.

When they went out to find one they were going to ride Jeeps. But didn't want anyone to see. Took a transport instead. Peck. We'll throw him in the back. If anyone asks, we'll say we're moving supplies. But no one did. Went out. Got one. A prisoner. Brought him back.

Mark said hey, man. You want to?

What?

Drive it.

It was awesome. Black. Looked brand new. They got discontinued. Heard that. Couldn't remember where. Maybe the radio. Or someone told him. Wasn't sure how it looked so new. Someone famous? Probably not. From Boston probably. Mass plates.

Whose is it?

No idea. Never saw it here before.

No man. You take it.

I've driven one. You should.

So he did.

It was okay.

Around the building. Could've gone straight into a bay. Didn't think anyone would mind. Wouldn't show on the odometer.

Drove in. Got out.

Didn't know what he did. Or didn't do. Thought it was the same. Mark showed him. A bunch of times every day. Remembered going through all the steps in his head.

Usually news radio for Doris. Wasn't there. Music instead. Echoes all over the garage. "You Shook Me All Night Long." Loved it before he went. Him and Artie. Driving to Boston. To see the Sox. Or just around town. Turn it up! Echoed in the garage. All songs echoed there. Made it sound like an arena. Felt the music in his chest. System of a Down. Saw them at the Civic Center. Sounded like that. Echoey. He wanted to see AC/DC. Angus. Be right up front.

The drive. The room.

The desert.

AC/DC.

We have to get them back. For what they did. Show them.

Behind his eyes.

Oh shit.

Oh shit oh shit.

Keep it together man. Keep it together. Don't freak out. Don't let them see. They think it's cool. You love this song. Great song. Want this job. She was a fast oh god machine driving Peck his head man keep it together. Follow the steps do your job she kept the motor together clean keep it together the lift. Hummer. Transport. The lift change keep it together.

Hit the button. Started moving up.

Then a second where he saw and knew but couldn't move and felt his mouth go noooooo like in a movie when someone shoots and someone else jumps in front of the bullet. It wasn't like that. He knew. One second alive. The next dead. Head a red and gray cloud. Metal taste. His buddy got shot and they went out to get one of them. Take a prisoner. And they got him and fucked with him so bad the broomstick the pig impersonation Peck and his video camera they hit him and kicked him pissed all over him his face all he knew in English was please please didn't know if he was on camera probably was kicking the guy pissing on him and when they were done with the prisoner they went to take him back and he got shot right in the leg they all got shot ambushed so worried about dumping the guy they weren't careful weren't paying attention oh God Peck his head was there one second not there the neck brains all over him tasted like metal head there then nothing his head was nothing but a gray cloud blood tasted like metal in his mouth Peck's brains in his mouth please oh please.

But the Hummer was like that. In the air. Then fell. Landed on the back bumper. A huge CRASH. Breaking glass. Echoed. And there was Ahmed. Mark said he came in Thursdays.

Watching him drop a Hummer off a lift.

And not just a new Hummer. One with Mass plates. A Masshole's Hummer.

Ahmed yelled and yelled. Everyone stopped. Mark first, then him. I can't believe Sheila would recommend someone as incompetent as you. You're fired. Hopefully your pay will cover the damage you caused to this car.

Ahmed poked him in the chest. Leave the shirt. It's mine.

He'd call Sheila. Every garage in town. Do not hire Royal Eggleton.

Walked home. Freezing. No idea what to do.

Letter on the kitchen table. Nothing else.

Sat there. Shaking. Realized he had been since the garage. Since before the Hummer started to slip from the lift.

Didn't know how long he sat.

Needed something. Didn't know what to do. No money. Check gone. None coming in. Had to find something. Had to.

At some point he watched himself pick up the phone. Called the office. It's Roy Eggleton, his voice said. I need an appointment. My benefits ran out. I need to pay the bills. No money. Help.

They told him Monday, nine a.m.

Hoped to get in today. Friday. Had to wait all weekend.

They had to have something. Could go around to garages and apply. But Ahmed would call them all. Do not hire Royal Eggleton.

No construction. No garages. No factories. No call centers. No security. No groundskeeping. Not in the winter.

Didn't know what else to do.

Sat watching himself for a long time.

Back to normal after hours. Back.

Went to the library.

Looked at the want ads. Nothing. Office jobs. Nurses. Nothing he could do. Got on a computer. No email. No one wrote to him. No friends on PalCorral.

The library closed. He went home. Heated beans. Made Minute Rice. Ate. Not much food left. Or money. Get more beans. Rice. Cheapest food. Ramen. Getting sick of it. But needed to eat cheap. Couldn't remember the last time he ate at a restaurant. That ice cream the other day. Five bucks. Twenty ramen. Each beer, twelve packages after tip. But he needed beer. To play. Couldn't just go in. Needed to have one. Look like he belonged. A prop. Like this guy's not drinking? Just playing pool? I can't play a hustler. Had to look right. Weekends especially. People playing on weekends. He'd make some money.

Waited.

Missed baseball. Something to do. On in the background. Paying attention was hard before. Worse since he got back. Didn't know why. Maybe hearing. Listening. Hard to shake. Like finding himself on the ground when cars backfired. Still happened. Hard to sleep. Hard to read. Waiting for something. Always distracted. Didn't have to be. But couldn't stop. Reading gave him a headache. Top of his brain. Always thinking of something else. Pool was easy. Different shots. Fixing cars. Little things. Each nut. Bolt. Belt. Newspapers, no. Hard stringing words together. Couldn't remember the one before.

Hard concentrating on anything. After Peck. Long. The video. College Boy gone. Always knew. Would have said something. Like hey. Those pictures. Guy with the hood. Electrodes. Remember? You want that? Aw, heck, Peck would have said. You're right. We don't want this getting out. But College Boy got hit. Wasn't bad. Hospital, rehab. Flew back. No one there to say anything. Even though they all knew what College Boy would say. And did it anyway. Recorded him. For personal use, Peck said. My phone. And you know I'm not showing it to no TV channel. Relax. He laughed.

But then Peck. And Long. There one minute. Next, covered. Blood. Tasted like metal. Frick on the ground. Blood. His and Peck's and Long's. Couldn't hear anything. Prisoner running away. Blindfolded, hands tied. Hadn't tied legs. Didn't know why not. Cords in Frick's neck standing out, screaming. Always there in his head. Friends dead. Head a cloud. Frick never emailed. Or called. Donaldson. Waiting. Every day. Hoped he wasn't in the video. Tried to remember. Couldn't. So fast. Had been there. Remembered the phone. Might've been. Had the shovel. Blindfolded, bare feet. Dance, I said! You speaka English? Like in Westerns. Except Westerns had shooting. He didn't do that. Might hurt him. Didn't want to. Just scare him. Humiliate him. Peck, with the pig 'persination. So funny. Like *Jackass*.

Couldn't wait any more. Couldn't sit. Had to go. Grabbed his jacket and walked to Patterson's. Half-full. No one at the table. Practice.

Hello, Roy, Patterson said. How's the job?

Good, he said. Good.

Looking for some pool?

Yes, ma'am.

It's been quiet. Maybe later on.

Maybe, he said. Hope so.

Venerable?

Yes, please, he said. Thank you.

She gave him the beer. He paid, tipped. Brought it to the table. Out of quarters. No roll. Needed change. Got some. Seven dollars left. Lucky.

29.

Today sucked.

When I got to school everyone was pointing and whispering again, except worse than yesterday. Everything was on the news last night. It wasn't just Ross who got suspended, but he was the main one they talked about. I heard from Mary there were some shots of the house. She saw the whole thing. It talked about how Ross was being recruited before this. No schools have commented.

She said your brother's famous. I was like whatever. I wanted to hang out with her today but she had to go see her cousin. But tomorrow she'll be up at the quarries, so I'll see her more then.

But anyway. When I got up Ross wasn't around. Neither was Mom. Don was passed out on the couch, surrounded by cans. I didn't hear him come in last night. I was reading and then went to bed.

Some nerds in the hallway were talking about Ross today and I freaked out. One of them called my brother a druggie when I walked by so I punched him. His nose started bleeding. Blood was running all down his shirt. I thought it was kinda awesome. All day I thought I'd get called down to the office for that but I didn't. Don would beat the shit out of me. He might still because of what happened at work later.

The first person I saw was Dalton. He asked if I was okay. I said yeah. But everyone was looking at me. Jack and Paul both kept staring until I was like what?

Judy got off her shift and Gary started his.

I was on fry station. It was better than being on cashier, but not much better because I could still feel everyone's eyes on me all day. No matter where I go in town, someone is like I know her, whether it's because of my mom or her dumb boyfriend or my brother.

He fucked up his chance to get out of here. I shouldn't feel good about it, but I kinda do. Like, the only guy in town who could do something blows it, and I like it. I don't know. I guess I coulda gone to Nebraska to visit him or something. Or maybe he woulda bought us all cars and houses when he went pro. But now I guess he won't get to go. He'll be stuck here with the rest of us. Maybe he'll work at Burger Hut or in the mill or something. Or he'll have to join up. Whatever it is, he'll be thinking about how he used to play back in the day.

Anyway, I was doing fries and everyone who came in knew who I was because of my stupid brother. The shift changed and Gary was there behind me, really close, like not touching me but he might well have been. I could smell his coffee breath.

He walked away and I was trying to decide what to do when these kids over by the register started in on me. One of them said YOUR BROTHER'S A LOSER really loud in a fake cough. I stood and tried to look busy with the fries and they were like hey, we know you can hear us.

I could feel myself starting to cry. How stupid is that? Starting to cry even though I'm kinda glad my dumb brother won't get out. I had to bite my lip to keep from crying right there at the fry machine. Then the buzzer went off.

I couldn't move. It was buzzing and buzzing while I stood there trying not to cry. If I moved I knew I'd lose it. This one guy out there was talking really loud about my brother. I knew that if I moved I'd start bawling and those kids out there would win. And fuck that, you know? Fuck that. I'm not crying for them. So I finally got my shit together and turned around and gave them the finger. That made me feel a little better.

I took the fries out and they were a little browner than usual but I thought maybe they were okay so I dumped them in the tray and salted them like I'm supposed to.

Of course, Gary saw everything. He came over and stood real close like before and said Dixon, those fries cannot be served. I was like they're fine, they're just a little browner than usual. The crispy ones are the best. He said they are not fine. We have the highest standards of quality here and I was like yeah, yeah.

The kids were all still out there listening. Everyone probably was. And then he said on top of that, I saw an inappropriate gesture from you. I was like those kids were calling my brother a loser. I could feel myself starting to cry again and started to bite my lip. He said be that as it may, interacting with the customers in such a manner is completely inappropriate. I was like you don't understand. He said there is nothing to understand. You have acted inappropriately.

Without thinking, loud enough so everyone heard it, I said what do you want? You wanna see my tits again or something?

I could hear Dalton start laughing, then try to make it sound like he was coughing.

Gary turned bright red. If I wasn't so pissed it woulda been funny. Then he said you're fired.

I took off my stupid paper hat and threw it on the ground and yelled FUCK YOU at him. Then I went out and the kids were still there laughing and they started clapping. I yelled at them YOU FUCKING GOT ME FIRED even though I was tired of that stupid job anyway. I wasn't gonna tell them that.

The kid who talked the loudest was like why don't you have your brother get you a job dealing weed? Without even thinking I punched him. His nose started bleeding right there in Burger Hut. That was two people in one day whose noses I made bleed.

One lady in the dining room screamed. The kid went OH, YOU BROKE MY NOSE real loud in this funny voice and I was like don't be a little bitch. One of his friends grabbed me so I punched him, too. He didn't bleed or anything but he yelled and let me go.

Gary came out from the back and said Dixon, I have called the police. I said you're a creepy old perv. I could hear Dalton laughing in the back. He wasn't even trying to cough. Gary said leave the premises and never come back. You are banned from the Burger Hut for life. I was like oh, no! Banned from the Burger Hut! How am I gonna have healthy dining choices now? I could hear Dalton laughing even louder. Gary said if you're here when the police arrive I will have you arrested for trespassing, plus whatever charges your new friends care to bring up. When he said that the kids were like we're gonna get you thrown in jail and I was like shut the fuck up and took a step toward them. They flinched. The guy whose nose I guess I broke wasn't bleeding any more but he had all these Burger Hut napkins jammed up there.

I went back inside the work area and Gary was trying to yell at me except for some reason I guess he couldn't. He was all red and had this funny voice which I could tell was him being angry. He was all Dixon, I said you need to leave the premises imme-diately and I was like chill out, you old perv, I'm just getting my bag. So I walked by him into the locker room and got my back-pack. It was still pretty heavy because of everything inside. I was walking out when Dalton came over with his hand up and said you're a baller. I said thanks and high-fived him. The hand slap was really loud. Then I walked out past napkin nose. He was crying.

When I unlocked my bike I saw cop cars coming so I tried to act normal and biked away before they could get out.

I figured because I punched the kid and called Gary a perv I wouldn't get paid, so I wanted to find Ding to get rid of the laptop. I biked over to the L'il Bee.

I saw the cop car in the parking lot. It had its lights on.

Instead of stopping I biked by like nothing was wrong. It was parked next to Ding's car. A cop had him up against the hood.

What if Ding starts talking about all the stuff I brought him?

And what if he talks about Ross?

I circled back past on the other side of the road and biked to the Pines. I went into a house I've never used before. I propped the laptop up on a rock and set off a couple Silver Salutes I still had in my backpack. Then I did an M-80. But after all that it still kinda looked like a laptop. So I smashed the rest outside.

I hit it with a rock over and over again until it didn't look like anything. Just a pile. I could feel how cold the ground was through my stupid Burger Hut pants. My shoulders hurt when I was done and I was breathing heavy. I think I did a pretty good job—like if you didn't know it was a laptop you couldn't tell. I picked up the pieces and scattered them around.

It was starting to get dark so I got on my bike and headed back. It was too early to go home, but too dark to go to the quarry through the woods. I went by L'il Bee again to see if anyone was there. I didn't see anyone. I wish Mary didn't have to hang out with her cousin today.

Mom's car was in the driveway when I got back. I was like oh shit. Is she home early because I got fired? Or because of Ross's drug test? Or because Ding ratted him out?

Or me?

I wanted to get out of there but there was no place else to go. I thought I could at least get in the back way, so I took my bike around where I always do and locked it and tried to sneak in. But the door squeaked.

Mom and Don didn't care. Through the kitchen I could see Don yelling at the couch with Mom standing next to him. They didn't even know I was there.

Don was pissed. He was like it doesn't matter! Ross said come on, Don. They called after they heard about all this. They saw me on the news and watched those tapes we sent. Don was like that's not the point and Mom was trying to say stuff but they wouldn't let her. Ross said Colorado, Don. And Washington. Don said it's the principle of the thing.

Mom was like you two need to stop!

I tried to walk by without getting into the whole thing and Don said stop right there. I couldn't not, so I stood there and went what? Don said you must know by now that your brother is suspended. I said yeah, people have been giving me shit for it all day. Mom said Dixon, language, and Don said giving you shit? All the guys are gonna rag on me because my stepson didn't get to play in the State Championship because of some reefer. Ross said I'm not your stepson. Mom was like can you two just stop it? Ross pointed to Don and was like he's always calling me his stepson.

Don took a step toward Ross and said show some respect, you little prick. Then Ross pushed him backward and Mom started screaming.

I wanted to get out of there so I went through the living room and down the hall. Ross was staring at Don with his fists up and Mom was screaming stop, stop and Ross was like I'm not your stepson. I went and locked myself in my room. I could hear thumps and stuff like that.

There was too much yelling to read and I didn't want to talk about it yet because I thought if they heard my voice maybe they'd come in, so I sat on my bed and waited for it to be over. There was more thumping and yelling and then a door slammed, and another one.

He leaves soon. Dunno exactly when. Hopefully Mom grows a pair and kicks him out. But she never does. Me and Ross have to have him around for another few weeks. Then he'll be gone.

The kids at Burger Hut knew who I was before I quit, and before I punched them. Maybe they go to school with me. If they do they'll get me back. I'm not sure they'd hit a girl, but maybe.

And the job.

And Ding. I don't know what I'm gonna do for money.

I wish Mary were here.

30.

Zachariah had been so preoccupied with his idea of impressing Dixon Dove that he hadn't even thought about her locker.

Instead of locking his bike and using the side door, he took the direct route, past the new, young, security guard. Zachariah thought he looked familiar.

There she was, moving books from locker to bag.

Stupid. But he'd been thinking about his idea. And his bike ride. He knew he could put most of his weight on his cast, but thought it better not to. Biking with most of his weight on his right hand—the good one—wasn't difficult physically, but remembering not to fall into his normal two-handed stance took more concentration than he thought.

He felt himself freeze in the doorway at the sight of Dixon Dove. Somehow he kept moving. Head down, he walked by, hoping she wouldn't notice him—and hoping she would

She didn't.

* * *

He had it all figured out. Just a few pieces missing.

To impress her. Get her to like him. If he could do that, he could do anything. Write a better game show. Start a bakery. Get his dad to stop hitting him.

It seemed impossible initially, but he knew how.

* * *

At lunchtime he went straight to the library computers. It wasn't until the bell rang that he realized he'd forgotten to eat his chips and sandwich.

* * *

He went down to the basement when he got home. His dad had a workbench there that he never used, covered with power tools and half-full toolboxes.

Inside one, he found sanding belts. Sanding tape, too.

31.

WHAT THE HELL WAS THE NAME? Guy who sang high. Him. Song he did. Name not in the band. What was it?

So, Roy, the lady said. What do you think?

Should he say something? About the cast? She would see. Must've. And didn't say anything. But it was right there. On his lap. Heavy. Greenish mesh over plaster. Never had one before. Always thought just plaster. Covered with autographs. Friends. But green mesh. And no one to sign it. Could have her do it. She'd be the only one. Lady at the office. Got me the job. He'd let Artie sign if he wanted to. Mark. If he ever saw him again.

I could do that, he said.

Stand there. More to be seen than anything. Like MPs. Everyone knew. Go easy around MPs.

She started talking about his military experience blah blah training blah blah.

Was playing lefty. Getting better. Felt it. Practice. Might win more. Save righty. Third game. First two easy. Challenges. Stripes off a bumper. Solids off a ball. Hadn't done that in a while.

Played. Good game. Door opened. More people. Looked quick. Didn't recognize them. College age. Maybe they'd play.

"*It Keeps You Runnin'.*" The guy with the voice. Singing in his voice, "*It Keeps You Runnin'.*"

Roy?

Yes?

Are you with me?

Oh. Yes. Uh. I was just thinking. About how great the job will be.

Hoped he hadn't fucked it up.

Lady smiled. Very good. I hope you understand there are risks. Since the death of the previous security guard the district tried to cut the position, but apparently students have been wielding knives in plain view in the hallways.

I can do it.

So when can you start?

Right away. Today.

Couldn't believe the timing. Everything happened. Got fired, the bar, now bills, probably. Didn't know how that would work. And the lady didn't look like someone farted. First time.

I'm glad you called, she said. We had the position open up last week. You'll be perfect for it.

Wouldn't be that bad shooting lefty. Couldn't be, right? So good like that with pool. He could learn. Give him something else to do. Pool hard now. Could carve a notch into his cast. Might fuck it up. Or his hand. So going to the woods to practice would be great.

The gravel pit. Hadn't been for a long time. Not since before he left. Him and Artie. Bunch of bottles and cans in a row, one by one. He was better than Artie. Remembered that. Better at something than Artie. Now pool too. But then nothing. Artie, of course, cheered every time and yelled YEAH HAHA GET

'EM. And he meant it. Roy wished he could do that. Be like Artie. Cheer other people. Started to. Overseas. But was jealous. Sucked at first in Basic. Other people didn't have to clean shit. Jealous of that. But afterward he was in the middle. Not the best, not the worst. Blended in. Everything but pool. Felt people jealous of him. Over there. Here, just wanted to win money. Didn't rub it in people's faces. Knew what that was like. Artie was just like haha and not mad. Or jealous. Had everything going for him. Girlfriend, job.

Now he'd have one. Again. Wouldn't fuck it up.

W-2, I-9. Just filled that stuff out. Had all his papers. Would do it again. She said training would be short. Needed the position. Sudden vacancy and all. And the problems I mentioned, the knives. Roy tried to remember if there was a guard when he went to Armbrister High. Couldn't. But wasn't looking for one. Sometimes when you weren't looking for something you couldn't see it. Then you started and it was right there.

New song. Started slow. Then happy. Some lady. Foreign name. Dutch. Belgian. Something. Liked it okay. What was it called?

When it happened, the guy he didn't recognize said hey, can I get a game. He said sure. Let me just finish with these. The guy said okay and went to the bar. Came back with a beer.

Nothing from Ahmed. Was afraid. Thought a big envelope would come back with a bill. Letters from court. Or the guy. With the Hummer. Court summons. Something. But maybe not. Someone there could fix it for free. Mark. Dmitry. One of the other guys. Or the garage had insurance.

Didn't see how bad it was. Ahmed yelling, telling him he was fired. Take off the shirt. Then he left. Wasn't like it was plastic. One of those little cars, economy, the whole thing would have broke. Busted the frame. Irreparable. But a Hummer? Made of metal, right? Not plastic? Could withstand a fall? So maybe that was it.

Kept hoping for a check but knew one wouldn't come.

99 Red Balloons Go By. That was it.

Didn't tell her about the garage. Hadn't updated. Didn't think he needed to. Ahmed didn't know everyone. Garages he knew. Junkyards. Towing companies. Couldn't go everywhere. But he had kids. Patterson said that. At the Double Scoop. So a chance. But he got the job. Had it. She was giving it to him. Brought his paperwork in case. Sign the line. Get it done. Shouldn't worry.

Hand itched. Heard that meant healing. Didn't know which part was itching. Hard to tell. Felt the same, but knew it wasn't. Pins. How much did they cost? A lot. Get the same thing at the hardware store for a buck.

Didn't see them put in. Passed out. Didn't remember much. Remembered it happening, but not after that. Kinda remembered the hospital. Waking up and some nurse saying Royal, do you know where you are? Thought oh God I'm hit they got me and went back down. Brought himself down. Didn't want to deal. They told him afterward it was drugs. Made sense. But he still did it himself. Could have woken up. But didn't want to. Thought he was back there. Couldn't do that. Couldn't handle it. Being back. Had dreams like that sometimes. Woke up in a bunk in basic. Woke up in a bunk in the barracks. Woke up sleeping in the desert. Basic one was the worst. Had that one the most. Knew he wasn't supposed to be there. Told the DI. There's been a mistake. I'm not supposed to be here. Knew he was right. Knew he had already done everything. Been overseas. Been shot. Been discharged. But the DI wouldn't let him go. Had to do it all over again. Everything. New guys with him. Make friends with them. Go overseas with them. Watch them get hurt. Killed. Come back. Be broke. Never find a job.

Your time in the military makes you an ideal candidate, she said. He tried to pay attention as she talked but the song ended and a new one came on. Songs all the time. Everywhere. Couldn't ever escape. The news, he liked that. At the garage. People calling up to talk about it. Stuff that happened. He thought he could get used to it. Listened to sports talk radio sometimes. Liked that. Mut and Merloni. Good guys. Knew about sports stuff. Sox. Pats. Didn't make him feel dumb like the news stations did. At first. But he started to get it. Quick. Three days. Hated it at first, hung out with Mark. But he started to like it. Like hey, they talked about this stuff before. Some war, but not much. Mostly politics in the United States. And Europe. Wasn't bad. Kinda liked it. Mark asked him to do stuff and he did it and listened to the radio. Thought about news he'd learn like that. Hanging out in the garage, doing his job, listening to the news. Might be able to go to an expensive bar with Artie sometime and talk to ladies. Drink an expensive beer and say you know, this beer is very hoppy and exports are going up and some lady would say that's really interesting. I'm so interested in what you're saying.

Didn't know what this one was. Had heard it, but wasn't sure. Doo-doo (pause) doo-doo-doo-doo, doo-doo (pause) doo-doo-doo-doo, doo-doo (pause) doo-doo-doo-doo, doo-doo-dahh-hhhh. Didn't know.

Played good the first game. Almost won. Guy looked familiar. Wasn't talking much. Just your shot and stuff like that. Thought he had the guy on the ropes. But he fucked up. Missed a shot. Guy got it. Sank the eight ball.

Let's play again, the guy said. Roy said wanna play for the game? The guy said sure. Didn't try as hard. Made a lucky shot, missed a few he shouldn't've. Made sure to be angry when he missed close ones. Not real mad, but mad enough. Like frustrated. Then the guy said wanna play for money? Roy said sure. Lost that one. Did double or nothing, got him to go best of five. Switched hands.

Then the guy was like I need a beer and came back with five other guys. The ones who came in after.

One of them was familiar.

The one he was playing with said is this the guy?

Familiar guy said yeah. That's him. The hustler. Got a bunch of my money.

The guy he was playing with said we're gonna settle this outside.

Two pretty big guys. Two regular. If it was just the regular guys he might take them. Fight them. Or he might yell to Patterson CALL THE COPS. But the biggest guy stood back and took a knife out of his pocket. Far enough away from everyone so no one could see. Just him.

Knife guy said we're going outside. All of us.

So he had to go.

Three of them first, then him, then knife guy. Wished he opened a tab. Didn't. Paid as he went. With a tab Patterson might've gotten mad. Roy, you forgot to pay. Come out. Call the cops. Thought she probably did anyway. Who else would have? Not those guys. They took him around the corner. Dark there. No one could see. He'd have to thank her. Hadn't been back since. Why bother? No money. Couldn't play pool with a cast.

Kicked him in the nuts first. Went down. They knew how to do it. Then he felt boots kicking him. Hurt. Curled up. Covered his head. Yelling and kicking and calling him a motherfucker. Mostly got his legs. Balls aching into his stomach. His arms. But then hands on his wrist pulling his arm away from his head. Motherfucker thinking you're so smart switching hands? Crunch. Felt his hand go. Never felt pain like that. Even when he was shot. Screamed. Couldn't help it. Same thing again. Crunch. Didn't know what it was. Doctor said something harder than a foot. A boot, maybe? Didn't know. Felt something warm on his face and thought oh no I'm bleeding but it kept coming and wasn't blood thick and it stank and he knew it was piss. Before he passed out he thought they're humiliating me.

DI telling him he had to do it all again. Passed out. Woke up dry in a cast.

The pause. That's what made him know. Figure it out.

"Take It To the Limit." One more time. Old song. Didn't even know who it was. Or how he knew it. Just did.

So Roy, she said. When can you fill out the paperwork?

Now, he said. Right now. I brought everything. Just in case.

32.

TODAY WAS WORSE.

At school I saw Mary.

I wanted to tell her about everything that's been going on. The work thing sucked, but I knew she'd think it was funny. Or that she'd be happy I get to go to the game this weekend, like they said I would. When Steve said he'd see me next week I didn't believe it because I thought I could handle Gary. But they were right. I couldn't.

She was weird. Like she didn't want to talk to me.

I wanted to tell her about Ross and Don fighting. And Ding. I still don't know what that cop thing last night was about.

I saw her and said hey but she kept walking. I said hey again and she kept walking. I said hey and grabbed her. She spun around all mad and said keep your hands off me. I almost said something, like you never said that before, but I didn't. I thought about it first.

Then I said what's wrong?

She said you lied to me.

I was like what are you talking about? She said the knife. I asked if you always had it and you said yes.

I told her I never said that. I didn't tell her where I got it. Then I was like what's up with the knife, anyway? She said my cousin lost one that looked just like it. Ruby handle with a picture of an old car on it. He left it in his truck and when he got back from the store it was gone. And then it shows up on you. You're a liar and a thief and I never want to see you again.

I was like but I showed you the iPad! And I told you I got it from a car! And that wasn't a big deal, so the knife shouldn't be, either. It was a mistake. I'll give it to you so you can give it back. I took it out of my pocket and held it out and said here, take it. Take it! Give it back! I don't want you to be mad at me. I wanna hang out. I have so much to tell you.

But she was like I don't hang out with liars. Goodbye.

I was standing there holding the knife, thinking maybe I could give it back to her cousin myself and apologize and make everything okay, but I don't know who her cousin is. I thought maybe I could go to the same parking lot and find the truck and wait for him there.

Of course Trombley walked by. Right when I got to class I got called to the office.

Dr. Delacroix asked for the knife. I put it on his desk. He said no knives are allowed at school. Given your past, and the recent developments with your family, I think this is a good opportunity for you to go home and think about this rule for a week.

When he said that I was like oh fuck, suspension. I don't wanna stay home with Don. If I still had the job I could pick up extra shifts and say that I've been at school all day, or trade day for night or something. Instead I'm stuck at home. Don's gonna be wasted on the couch and get mean and hit me. And Mom's gonna be pissed. First Ross, then me in the same week.

And it sucks because I like the book. Today in class Merrill was talking about stuff and I didn't finish the reading last night because it was hard to concentrate, but I still understood what he was saying. Isn't that crazy? I followed along. So I guess I can finish it at home, but then I'll be done with it, and then what?

I saw Kelly later. She said how's work? I said I quit.

She said you quit?

I told her about the guys making fun of me, and about Gary.

She was like you probably don't want to think about football, right? Because of your brother? And I said I need to get out of the house.

I don't wanna go because of Mary, though. It'd be weird to see her and have her ignore me. Unless she shit talked me to everyone else.

Then she said will the quarry be okay? Because of Ding?

I told her about seeing him and the cop car. She told me he got busted.

Then she said Steve and Earl got hauled in, too.

I felt sick when she told me that. I tried to be cool, though, and ask what for. She said Ding is a major dealer. They were trying to get those guys to talk. But they didn't say anything.

What about me?

Would he rat me out? I never bought from him. But still. All the iPads and stuff.

And Ross!

He was in some deep shit even before Ding got busted.

But Ross would never rat out Ding. Would he?

Kelly kept talking for a while. I'm gonna meet her at the quarry. Hopefully Mary will be there. If not, I'll get wasted.

* * *

When I went back to the rack after school my bike was trashed. All the cords are cut and the wheels looked like someone jumped on them. Tires slashed.

* * *

It started raining when I walked home. Fucking figures. A shitty day, then I get rained on.

Don was sober when I got back.

He said sit your ass down right now. We need to talk.

I wanted to run. Or at least change into dry clothes. But I sat.

What the fuck is this about you getting fired?

I started to be like what are you talking about? But there was no way. So instead I said how did you find out?

He said the cops came by. You broke some kid's nose?

I said yeah.

And got fired?

Gary's a fucking perv.

He said you watch your mouth. Maybe if you had some manners none of this woulda happened. You ever think of that?

I started to say whatever, but I didn't want to get hit. So I said no.

He's pressing charges, you know. Assault. You're gonna get sent to juvie.

I was like am not and he said Dixon, they have video of you doing it.

There was nothing to say.

He said they're coming back soon. They want to talk to both of you. Your brother about some punk that got busted dealing grass, and you for breaking a kid's nose.

I sat there on the couch, dripping wet.

My bike getting fucked up really sucks. I'm gonna have to

hitch. I should be able to get rides. I know how to do it. And I know how to get money.

I wish I still had the knife. I might need it.

I'm gonna take all of Ross's weed with me. I can sell it.

It took me a while to find it. He had some good hiding places. Not as good as mine, though.

I'll leave him a note.

No, two.

33.

Zachariah kept a recipe window for Beef Wellington open as he searched.

He tried to imagine a beef tenderloin. A long, round slab of beef cooked in the oven was a far cry from steak tips or hamburgers.

He'd looked up the recipe after seeing the dish time and again on Pierre Lefevre's cooking show: beef covered in mustard and mushrooms, wrapped in pastry, and roasted in the oven. The technique mystified him. In his video, Pierre used plastic wrap—which he called "cling film"—to roll the ingredients into shape. Plastic wrap! He didn't know chefs used it to make dishes. For wrapping bowls or saving leftovers, sure. There had to be thousands of tricks like that he didn't know. How did people learn them? It wasn't the invention of the tricks, he thought, so much as how they were used. Once he knew the techniques behind his ideas, he could use them over and over again. Improve on them, even, in the way he did with bread. Improvise a little, maybe.

In the recipe on-screen he recognized the pattern.

His mom had taught him the chocolate sauce recipe before she left. His memories of her were largely based more on impressions than events—he had a feeling when he thought about his mother, but not a wide bank of experiences he could visualize.

He did remember being in the kitchen with her, though. She had two of those triangle candy bars. He'd never seen them before that. Zachariah asked if he could eat one.

We're going to use this for sauce, Zachie, she said.

Sauce?

For these brownies I'm making.

What was the occasion? He didn't think his mom and dad had a lot of money for sweets, even when they were still together. Still, he distinctly remembered her warming cream in a pot, then pouring it hot onto the triangular blocks of chocolate at the bottom of the bowl (save two segments, which he and his mom ate). And he remembered also whipping the mix, then pouring it onto the tray of brownies. Together they had spread it on with a rubber spatula.

Shortly afterward she was gone.

For years, Zachariah wondered why she hadn't taken him along. He was stuck with his dad, who forced him to wear paint to football games, made him do all the cooking (which he liked) and cleaning (which he didn't, despite his familiarity with all the cleaning products under the kitchen sink), and beat him with tennis balls—or worse—as punishment for tiny transgressions.

He hadn't spent much time thinking about why she left. He didn't remember his father hitting her. But he must have.

Zachariah wondered what it would be like to see her again. She'd drop by his mansion in California and call him Zachie the way she used to. He'd cook her lunch in his giant gleaming kitchen and ask her why she hadn't taken him along. He'd tell her how Paul had broken his arm over a bottle of barbecue sauce and made him lie about falling down the basement stairs. And she'd feel horrible and beg for forgiveness.

Ms. Petrie walked by. She stopped and looked at the screen. "What's that?"

He had been thinking so intently of his mother coming to visit his mansion that he hadn't had time to think about the computer. But he'd been safe about it. Even if he hadn't been, he could've said something about chores, maybe. Cleaning.

He pointed to the bigger window. "Beef Wellington."

"Are you watching Julia Child?"

"Pierre Lefevre," he said. "*Chef Wars*."

"I've heard of him," she said. "The French chef."

Zachariah nodded.

"Do you like to cook?"

"Baking is my favorite," he said. "But I like cooking, too."

"Is that what you want to do? When you grow up?"

"I don't know," he said. "I like cooking a lot. Especially baking. But I'd like to write game shows. I know it's hard to make it in Hollywood, so having a bakery will be my fallback."

"That's very sensible," she said. "A lot of times students get so wrapped up in thoughts of fame that they don't have fallbacks."

* * *

He mixed on the workbench, letting his mind wander. It was a lot like taking a shower—he always had great ideas when his body was focused on a task that didn't take up much space in his head.

On the floor was his backpack, embroidered with his initials. He hadn't thought anything of them for the longest time— L.L.Bean always monogrammed—but they had become the focal point of taunts after he had been kicked in the nuts. The "ZT" stitched in white, previously ignored, became the root of jokes about zits—Zit Tietz, Piss Zits. He knew the bag was an expensive one, so removing them was not an option, unless coupled with a beating from his father.

There was no mistaking it. He was the only student in school whose first name began with a Z.

34.

Loved it.

Couldn't believe it.

Everything was going right.

Armbrister High. Hated it the first time.

Should've gone voc. Would've changed everything. Never would've gone over. Gotten training. Learned cars for real. Gotten a job. Instead of going overseas and getting fucked up and coming back and dropping a Hummer off a lift and hustling pool and getting stomped and pissed on.

Straight to a garage. A job. No basic. No heads that were clouds. Could still listen to music. Sox games with Artie. No shitty apartment. Live with Auntie Blake. Save money. Get an apartment. A car. Everything easier. No pool. No pins.

Scared since then. Stupid. Knew how to fight. Knew how to take care of himself. Had been shot. Lived through it. Killed guys. Never scared since he got back. Not once. Not counting after dreams. But now all the time. Couldn't help it. Held a knife to him. Made him go outside Patterson's. To piss on him. Couldn't move right hand. In cast. Doctor said it might not recover. The good one. Had to fill out paperwork with his left. Looked like a little kid wrote it.

Wasn't sleeping. Heard noises. Weren't there before. Or didn't notice them. Maybe there before. But kept waking up. Sitting up in bed. Yelling. WHO'S THERE? Falling back asleep. Basic dream. Over and over. Standing with everyone. Heads into clouds. One after the other. Always woke up before it was his turn. But had to watch. Came back. Could sleep again. Never could over there. Barracks, maybe. But that was it. Slept lots at the hospital when he got back. And looking for work.

Still kept the hours. Mostly. Bed after the Sox during the season, up at five thirty. After cloud head dreams. Or basic. Or both.

But the job.

Stood by the door. Said hello. Kids liked him.

First day some kids came up. Tuesday. Tough. Remembered it: gotta give the new guy shit. Shut them up quick. They said take your gun out. He said no. They said ever kill anyone with it? He said no, not with this one. Since then every day they came by and said wassup, Roy?

Easy job. Stand by the door. Say hello. Break up fights. Teachers too scared to. Used to be shop teachers. Where were they? Happy about the work. Just wondering.

Broke one up. Two girls. Down in voc. Bitch fight, they called it. In the stairwell. One girl kicking another. Walked down there. Got in the middle. Didn't touch either. Not supposed to. Put his hands on his hips. Yelled STOP IT RIGHT NOW. Everyone looked at him.

They stopped.

They listened to him.

It was great. Walked halls a lot. Got paid. Made sure everything was okay. Didn't keep the same times or routes. Didn't want them to figure it out. Because they would. Like deer in the woods. Sometimes cafeteria, sometimes door. No pattern.

Funny. Most of his teachers gone. Only been a few years. New staff. Didn't know any students. Wasn't much difference between them and him. But they looked young. Like really. Smart kids especially. Didn't have to worry. Clean hands. Oh no, I might not get into my first choice. No jobs. No worries. Couldn't believe how little they looked. Even shop kids. Tough. But they'd get jobs. Smart kids, they'd go to college, not find anything. Worry. Get old fast. Maybe go fight. Hoped not, but still. The voc kids, jobs. Pay up front: have a hard time, then go to a garage or something.

Did he used to look that little? Went home one day. Got out his yearbook. Looked at his picture. Couldn't believe it. Just a few years ago. A lot since then. The garage, looking for a job. The hospital. Getting shot. Basic. Looked at himself in the mirror. So many lines on his face. Standing in the desert. Felt older than he looked. And thought how he looked old. Especially every day at school.

Saw the fat kid. The one with the body paint. And from the ice cream store. Of course he saw a fat kid eating ice cream. Voc kid. Couldn't believe it. Fat kids never did voc. Got eaten alive there. But the fat kid did voc. Cooking. Chef coat, apron. Covered with flour or something. Made sense. Kid like that, he liked eating. Huge backpack full of books, every day. Kept an eye on him. Liked the kid. Reminded Roy of himself.

Looked good. Not like fat. Like happy. Didn't seem to mind. Kids gave him shit. Said shit. Roy couldn't say anything. Wanted to. Knew that would make it worse. Like the cop likes you. Get called a fag and shit. Didn't want to make it worse. But shit rolled off him. Like it was no big deal. Big backpack full of books, kids talking shit, just smiled and walked by. Wondered what he was thinking about. Cake, probably. Laughed when he thought that. Cracked himself up. Kids walking by just looked at him.

Whatever. Didn't matter. Thought it was great. Funny joke. Seriously, though. What was it? Wasn't like he just discovered cake. If that's what it was. Something changed since the game. Got more confidence. Maybe threw it to some girl. Probably not. But hoped that he did. He'd had to wait. Until basic. Thought about high school. Would things have been different? Maybe. Or not. Everyone gave him shit for other stuff. Mom, mostly. Never that virgin shit. But he was scared they would. Wouldn't be able to say anything back. Fat kid? So much shit. Someone would say something. Be like hey, fat kid. Ever kiss a girl? So maybe he pulled it off. Made out with some fat chick. Hoped so. Go, fat kid. Might ask someone his name. Hank the janitor. Delacroix. Someone. Be like hey, who's the happy fat kid?

35.

Sorry about everything.

Say you didn't know

I left a note.

36.

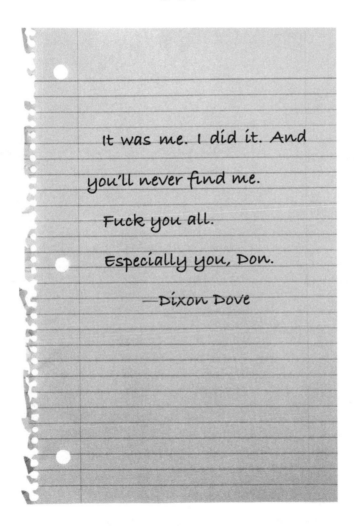

It was me. I did it. And

you'll never find me.

Fuck you all.

Especially you, Don.

—Dixon Dove

37.

Zachariah walked to school. He'd had to leave earlier than when he rode his bike, but he'd been so excited the previous night that he barely slept, out of bed a full hour before his alarm went off. After a bowl of cereal and a shower, his father still snoring away in his bedroom, Zachariah decided to work on *Love Balloon*, even though he had thrown out the cake scene.

The ending was the best part.

He wanted a regular guy to win. Not one of the strikers who looked like an underwear model. But luck of the draw was part of it. Part of everything. If Armbrister hadn't played Enoch on a Saturday afternoon, his dad might not have decided to celebrate a blowout by grilling. Paul Tietz would not have taken Zachariah to buy barbecue sauce. Dixon Dove would not have dumped barbecue sauce over Zachariah's head.

And if none of that had happened, Zachariah thought he would have gone on pretending that he had powers, playing defense rather than running with the ball.

He saw the pattern in himself because of Dixon Dove.

The ending had never changed. He had the idea for the final scene before he knew what the rest of the show would be like.

He then built his challenges so the finale of the first season could happen.

It was his dad who gave him the idea. In front of a baseball game on the couch, he sat with a glossy magazine and a stack of papers on a TV tray. It looked to Zachariah as if he were studying for a test.

Zachariah blurted out, "Dad, what are you doing?" He should have thought before he spoke, but was so surprised to see Paul doing anything but drinking and watching TV that he was caught off guard.

"Come here for a sec," his dad said.

Uh-oh.

Zachariah did.

"The guys at the mill put a fantasy league together."

He saw football players stretched horizontally to catch passes on the magazine's pages.

"I have to figure out my picks for the draft."

Zachariah was confused. "Draft like war?"

His father laughed. Zachariah couldn't remember him in such a good mood. "Maybe. Everyone takes turns picking a player."

"That's not fair," Zachariah said.

"Why not?"

"The first guy always gets the best pick."

"We're doing a snake draft."

"Snake?"

"Like an 'S.' There're twelve guys, so it goes one through twelve, then twelve through one. Like that."

Zachariah liked the idea of a snake draft. Being picked first in gym was the best thing—it meant everyone wanted you on their team. And being picked last, of course, meant the opposite. He used to get picked solidly in the middle of the pack before he got kicked in the nuts. Then he was last, even though he was better than some of the kids who got chosen before him.

With the snake draft, the guys in the middle had the best chance. It wasn't about the best pick, maybe, as much as it was about making smart picks.

After two weeks of the football season his dad, who had picked in the middle, lost his fantasy quarterback to a broken leg.

While he was at school, rolling bread on a floured metal school table he had the idea.

A big field, with a target in the center.

Everyone would buy squares. He wasn't sure how, but he could figure it out. Some kind of auction.

Someone would pilot a balloon onto the target.

But the target square wasn't the best pick. What if the person in the balloon wasn't a very good pilot? Or if it was windy?

Zachariah thought it would be a girl. The bachelorette everyone competed to be with. She'd try to land in the target. But she wouldn't know much about balloons. She'd probably land somewhere other than the target.

Whoever had bought the square she landed on would live with her afterward.

Maybe the best square was the one furthest from the center.

There was no way of telling.

Zachariah liked the idea because a normal guy could win.

* * *

His walk hadn't taken much longer than a bike ride, despite the weight on his back. He could feel his heart thumping in his chest even before he left the house. Dixon Dove would love her present. And she'd tell everyone that Zachariah Tietz was okay.

They'd have a partnership—he would make new recipes for her, and she would make sure he could sit in the cafeteria and eat his lunch in peace.

And maybe she'd want to touch his boner again.

The usual comments about his weight, pissed jeans, and pukey shirt were hurled at him as he stood at the foot of Armbrister High's granite steps, one hand on each backpack strap. But he smiled honest smiles at his tormentors. It would all be over soon. Everything would change when he partnered with Dixon Dove. He wished he had figured everything out sooner.

He walked up the stairs and through the doors, past the new security guard.

He looked at Zachariah as if they knew each other.

Zachariah stood waiting, waiting for Dixon Dove to arrive, one hand on each strap. He didn't know what Dixon Dove's schedule was like. She had some class in the morning—he knew this from all the times he had come in the front door only to be accosted by her.

His mind raced as the owners of surrounding lockers dropped off jackets, switched books, and stowed lunches. Where was she?

His straps began to dig into his shoulders, despite his thumbs.

The pace of the hallway's flow of students quickened with the warning bell. He didn't want to be late for class, but he didn't want to lug the bomb around all day, either, waiting for Dixon Dove to arrive. It was too heavy.

Maybe she was running late.

The security guard gave Zachariah a look he couldn't figure out, then walked down the hall. Zachariah stayed where he was.

The class bell rang.

He waited.

A few kids he didn't know came in over in the next few minutes, each with the same frantic look.

He had rehearsed it in his head: Dixon, I want to make a deal with you. You've been picking on me. But you like fireworks. So why don't I make them for you? Here's a sample. In exchange, you can stop picking on me, and make sure everyone else does, too.

And she'd say: How'd you learn how to make fireworks, Tietz?

He thought about telling her the truth: that something had changed when she dumped Slow Bull over his head. But he didn't think he should tell anyone about that. It was his: the change, and the aftereffects.

He thought about telling her the process: I did some research and found out that it's not hard to make bombs. I had all the ingredients in the house, mostly in kitchen cleaners. I wasn't sure about aluminum oxide, but my dad had sanding discs in our basement.

Instead, he thought he might try to sound mysterious. Like a character on a TV show: Well, I can bake bread. It's not that different.

He'd get in trouble if he skipped class. And his dad might hit him. The cast wouldn't stop beatings.

He'd leave it in Dixon Dove's locker.

But if he did that, she might find it and hurt herself. He wasn't sure exactly how strong it would be, but it was pretty big—he'd tripled the recipe he found online.

He would put it in her locker and make sure he disconnected the batteries. She'd know it was from him because of his initials monogrammed on the backpack.

But what if she didn't see them? Or didn't get the message? He hadn't known Ross Dove was her brother—maybe she wouldn't know the backpack was his.

He'd leave a note. Then, when she found it, he could show her how to hook the batteries back up—or, better yet, they could go to one of the Whispering Pines houses and set it off there.

Dixon Dove's locker opened easily. It was empty, save for some crumpled fast food wrappers at the very bottom.

He knew he was at the right one. He always saw her by her locker in the morning. Why was it empty?

The halls were silent. Everyone was in class.

He didn't want to carry the bag around. He'd put it in the locker, then find her.

It took a few pushes, but he was just able to wedge his bag in.

He unzipped the top and reached in to check the battery pack. His last thought, as he noticed the scent, before the explosion, was maybe the quarry—

38.

HEARD IT GO OFF DIDN'T SEE it and when it did he was lost he knew where his feet were leading him but he wasn't moving them like he was watching himself Peck Long feet carrying him paper everywhere moving slow like snowflakes to the ground no sound like snow falling everything quiet the only things moving paper old bags Burger Hut everything else still Peck oh God no screams nothing nothing but quiet blood everywhere splattered on lockers drops why wouldn't they fall hanging there huge drops how could there be snow a hundred and twenty degrees couldn't do it all again didn't want to go back oh God Long no but there he was except he wasn't back watched himself fall down like he was shot smell in the air metal in his mouth he was back knew the smell never went away always there dented doors all down the hall and blood huge drops hanging there off door vents people yelling oh God Roy what is it what's the matter and he watched himself try to speak nothing came out no sound what's the matter we need to find Roger that and he couldn't do anything oh my God is he hurt what happened what is this call an ambulance 911 couldn't move blood not moving paper hanging in the air like a cloud a gray cloud head cloud it would go away in a second everything would move and Long would be gone dead and Peck oh God Peck would be gone drop to the ground like a sack of potatoes didn't know how it could be this bad again again under his knees not sand bleeding everywhere hanging there that second oh God what happened is everyone okay no Peck why did he agree The Motor Clean hanging there just hanging—

39.

Why'd you set it off?

I don't know what the fuck you're talking about.

Come on. You disappear the same time a bomb goes off in your locker and you don't know what I'm talking about?

What?

You're not gonna win any Academy Awards, honey.

A bomb?

Stop playing dumb. You're wasting our time.

No. I'm serious. A bomb? How big?

Big enough to get you a murder charge.

Murder?

Don't act like you don't know.

I have no fucking idea!

Not even enough to do dental records. All we have is embroidery from a backpack. "ZT." Know him?

The fat kid?

His dad's drinking himself into a stupor right now. Because of you. And the poor bastard who's the security guard thinks he's back in Afghanistan.

The old guy?

Just hired a new guy. He got a Purple Heart in Afghanistan. A war hero.

It wasn't me! I didn't do any of that.

You're dead to rights, honey.

Jesus.

We have your confession.

What confession?

Look at this:

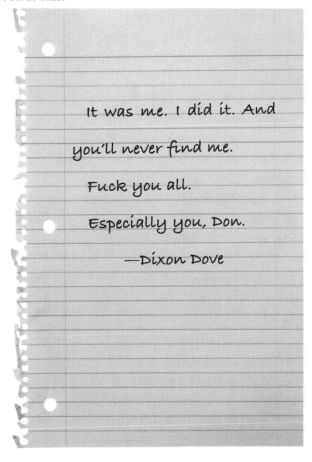

It was me. I did it. And

you'll never find me.

Fuck you all.

Especially you, Don.

—Dixon Dove

No. It's not—

You're fucked, girlie. You'll hang. People will cheer.

That's not it.

We found it at your house.

No. That note was about something else.

What?

I don't want to talk about it.

. . .

Look, that was about something else.

Reads like a confession to me. Case closed.

Listen, I—. My brother. Do you know about him?

Big football star.

He failed a drug test. There was a reporter.

Don't bullshit us, honey. We've got you.

No. And these kids were giving me shit about it. At Burger Hut. Where I used to work. They must have footage of it, right?

We don't want to hear it.

My mom's boyfriend said there was footage.

Put a sock in it.

And there was this girl. Mary.

You're really reaching now.

Look, I don't know about any bomb. I left because of all that stuff I told you about.

For where?

Boston.

Didn't get very far, did you?

Hitching isn't as easy as I thought.

The bomb was in your locker. And you left the note.

But there's another note. To my brother.

Sure there is.

And did you find the tape?
Excuse me?
The tape. My journal.
We didn't find any tape.
It's all on there. You haven't listened to it?

Acknowledgments

I STARTED THIS ONE ON SEPTEMBER 9, 2010 in Amherst, MA, right after I began my commute to Lowell, MA five days a week, ninety minutes each way.

The title *Swing State*—better than "Armbrister," a pre-Middlebrooks baseball interference in-joke—came to me in the shower sometime in 2012 at our new apartment in Belchertown, MA. I finished the sixth and more or less final draft at the big house in Orono, ME August 1, 2013, after two months of doubles bookending the Monsters of Talk tour.

Thank you to my amazing wife Rebecca Griffin for all her love and patience.

Peter Carlaftes and Kat Georges continue to believe in me, despite the fact that I'm a Red Sox fan.

Much respect to all the bookstores, galleries, living rooms, and basements that hosted readings on my Hidden Wheel tour: Rachel and Benn at Atomic Books; Aaron and Book Thug Nation; Black Wine; Pete Camerato and Pillowman; Chop Suey Books; Chris Dooley, Meghan Minior, and all at Flywheel; Valerie Leavy and Satellite 66; Megan London and all at Main Street Music Studios; Midtown Scholar; Megan and Dexter

Murphy; Papercut Zine Library; Gina Quaranto and Blackbird Studios; Liz and all at Quimby's; The Regulator Bookstore; Liberty and RiverRun Bookstore; Laurie Steelink and Track 16 (RIP); Liz at Stories; Txotuo and Sub-Mission Gallery; Eric Truchan and Rehab House; Maggie and all at Wonder Root; and Dani and Emily of Word Portland.

Beta readers: James Brophy, Jen Grosso, and Ed McNamara, Broderick Lang, Katie Lattari, Ben Stein.

Thanks to friends and family, pets included. Dr. Damian Adshead, Momi and Ramsay Antonio-Barnes, Tyler Babbie and Kate Kenderish, Billy Babbitt, Austin Bagley, the staff of the Belchertown Post Office, Tim Berrigan, Black Wine, Whitney Erin Boesel, Casey Boyd and Becky Cyr, Julie Burrell, Tobias Carroll and Vol. 1 Brooklyn, Coastwest Unrest, Marc "Gus" Desgroseilliers, Todd Dills and the 2nd Hand, Mike Faloon, Shelly Fank and Tim O'Neill, Ray and Kathy Fournier, Duane Gorey, Jay Grant, Great Western Plain, Ned Greene and Eliza Burke-Greene, Dave Griffin, Russ Griffin, Broseph Grillo and Hilary Preston, Emma Howes, Duncan Wilder Johnson, Kickstarter Muster Roll, Dave Kress, Kathy and Jerry Lacroix, Rich and Jackie Ladew-Tang, Dave Lawton, Miriam Leibowitz, Karen Lillis, Heather and Andy Malenke, Sam McPheeters, Paige and Lily Mitchell, Dan Moellering and Courtney Davis, Lisa Panepinto and Ryan Roderick, Rachel Perry and Rob Bergen, The Pichettes, Sammy Ponzar, Mike Powers, Brendan Emmett Quigley and Liz Donovan, Amber Porter and Ramsay Tatawi, Adra Raine, Steve Reynolds, Maggie Sabo, Kevin Shine and the ShineTones, Spippy, Taiwan Typhoon, Lori Timm, Tooth and Germ, Wah-Tut-Ca Scout Reservation, Tommy Walsh and Marna Eckels, Mike Watt, and you.

Molly T. Bunny—aka Cabildo—1997–2013.

Rest in Peace: Jon Cook and Jason Noble.

I'd love to read in your town/at your bookstore/in your living room/at your school, etc. Get in touch: michaeltfournier@gmail.com, and/or PO Box 784, Belchertown, MA 01007.

Now go start your own _____!

About the Author

MICHAEL T. FOURNIER IS A WRITER/CRITIC/MUSICIAN, and the author of two novels: *Hidden Wheel* (Three Rooms Press, 2011) and *Swing State* (Three Rooms Press, 2014), as well as *Double Nickels on the Dime* (33 1/3 Series/Bloomsbury Academic), a book-length discussion of the 1984 Minutemen album of the same name. He is founder and co-editor of *Cabildo Quarterly*, a broadsheet literary journal. His writing has appeared in the the *Oxford American*, *Vice*, *Pitchfork*, and the *Boston Globe*. He lives in Western Massachusetts with his wife Rebecca and their cat.

Recent and Forthcoming Books from Three Rooms Press

PHOTOGRAPHY-MEMOIR

Mike Watt
On & Off Bass

FICTION

Ron Dakron
Hello Devilfish!

Michael T. Fournier
Hidden Wheel
Swing State

Janet Hamill
Tales from the Eternal Café
(Introduction by Patti Smith)

Eamon Loingsigh
Light of the Diddicoy

Richard Vetere
The Writers Afterlife

DADA

Maintenant:
Journal of Contemporary
Dada Art & Literature
(Annual poetry/art journal,
since 2008)

MEMOIR & BIOGRAPHY

Nassrine Azimi and
Michel Wasserman
Last Boat to Yokohama:
The Life and Legacy of
Beate Sirota Gordon

Richard Katrovas
Raising Girls in Bohemia:
Meditations of an American
Father; A Memoir in Essays

Stephen Spotte
My Watery Self:
An Aquatic Memoir

SHORT STORY ANTHOLOGY

Have a NYC:
New York Short Stories
Annual Short Fiction Anthology

PLAYS

Madeline Artenberg &
Karen Hildebrand
The Old In-and-Out

Peter Carlaftes
Triumph For Rent (3 Plays)
Teatrophy (3 More Plays)

MIXED MEDIA

John S. Paul
Sign Language:
A Painters Notebook

TRANSLATIONS

Thomas Bernhard
On Earth and in Hell
(poems by the author
in German with English
translations by Peter Waugh)

Patrizia Gattaceca
Isula d'Anima / Soul Island
(poems by the author
in Corsican with English
translations)

César Vallejo | Gerard Malanga
Malanga Chasing Vallejo
(selected poems of César Vallejo
with English translations and ad-
ditional notes by Gerard Malanga)

George Wallace
EOS: Abductor of Men
(poems by the author in English
with Greek translations)

HUMOR

Peter Carlaftes
A Year on Facebook

POETRY COLLECTIONS

Hala Alyan
Atrium

Peter Carlaftes
DrunkYard Dog
I Fold with the Hand I Was Dealt

Thomas Fucaloro
It Starts from the Belly and Blooms
Inheriting Craziness is Like
a Soft Halo of Light

Kat Georges
Our Lady of the Hunger

Robert Gibbons
Close to the Tree

Israel Horovitz
Heaven and Other Poems

David Lawton
Sharp Blue Stream

Jane LeCroy
Signature Play

Philip Meersman
This is Belgian Chocolate

Jane Ormerod
Recreational Vehicles on Fire
Welcome to the Museum of Cattle

Lisa Panepinto
On This Borrowed Bike

George Wallace
Poppin' Johnny

Three Rooms Press | New York, NY | Current Catalog: www.threeroomspress.com
Three Rooms Press books are distributed by PGW/Perseus: www.pgw.com